Out Of The Frying Pan...

"You're a woman who doesn't take chances."

"And you're a man who's accustomed to taking them."

"Going to spend your whole life looking for a sure thing?" he asked, green eyes steady.

"Perhaps," Rani said coolly. "What about you? Going to spend your whole life leaping from one job, one adventure, to another?"

"People change, Rani."

"When?"

"When they find what they're looking for."

"I'd have to be awfully sure," she said cautiously.

"Before you'd take a chance on a man?"

"Yes."

"I realize my track record isn't exactly reassuring."

"You're right."

"But I'm not a boy. I've been looking for something for a long time. Something it takes a man to recognize."

"You think you've found it?"

"I think so. But the lady is going to have to take a chance, too, before either of us can be certain."

Dear Reader,

Welcome to Silhouette! Our goal is to give you hours of unbeatable reading pleasure, and we hope you'll enjoy each month's six new Silhouette Desires. These sensual, provocative love stories are both believable and compelling—sometimes they're poignant, sometimes humorous, but always enjoyable.

Indulge yourself. Experience all the passion and excitement of falling in love along with our heroine as she meets the irresistible man of her dreams and together they overcome all obstacles in the path to a happy ending.

If this is your first Desire, I hope it'll be the first of many. If you're already a Silhouette Desire reader, thanks for your support! Look for some of your favorite authors in the coming months: Stephanie James, Diana Palmer, Dixie Browning, Ann Major and Doreen Owens Malek, to name just a few.

Happy reading!

Isabel Swift
Senior Editor

SDRL-7/85

STEPHANIE JAMES
Green
Fire

Silhouette Desire
Published by Silhouette Books New York
America's Publisher of Contemporary Romance

SILHOUETTE BOOKS
300 East 42nd St., New York, N.Y.   10017

Copyright © 1986 by Jayne Krentz, Inc.

ISBN: 0-373-05277-4

First Silhouette Books printing May 1986

America's Publisher of Contemporary Romance

Printed in the U.S.A.

Books by Stephanie James

Silhouette Desire

Corporate Affair #1
Velvet Touch #11
Lover in Pursuit #19
Renaissance Man #25
Reckless Passion #31
Price of Surrender #37
Affair of Honor #49
To Tame the Hunter #55
Gamemaster #67
The Silver Snare #85
Battle Prize #97
Body Guard #103
Gambler's Woman #115
Fabulous Beast #127
Night of the Magician #145
Nightwalker #163
The Devil to Pay #187
Wizard #211
Golden Goddess #235
Cautious Lover #253
Green Fire #277

Silhouette Romance

A Passionate Business #89

Silhouette Special Edition

Dangerous Magic #15
Stormy Challenge #35

Silhouette Intimate Moments

Serpent in Paradise #9
Raven's Prey #21

STEPHANIE JAMES

readily admits that the chief influence on her writing is her "lifelong addiction to romantic daydreaming." She has spent the last nine years living and working with her engineer husband in a wide variety of places, including the Caribbean, the Southeast and the Pacific Northwest. Ms. James currently resides in California.

One

―――

His eyes were the color of the green stone in the ring on her hand. Rani Garroway registered that fact in the same instant she realized she'd opened the door to the wrong man. She was startled off balance and oddly shocked. Not just because she'd made a mistake in opening the door, but because of those eyes. The wind howled in the darkness beyond her doorstep, driving the rain through the tall pines and sturdy fir trees. The stranger didn't vanish with the next crackle of lightning. He continued to stand there in front of her, looking like a battle-scarred alley cat demanding shelter from the storm. His green eyes locked with hers.

"I'm sorry," Rani managed, wondering what to do next. "When I heard your knock I assumed you were someone else." Then a sense of self-protection came into play. The local mountain community, normally quiet, was filled with hunters arriving for the fall deer season. That meant a lot of strangers in the area. Armed strangers. Strangers who often mixed guns and alcohol. Her best bet was to make sure this man knew she wouldn't be alone for long. "I'm expecting someone else, you see. He'll be here any moment."

The man ignored her comment the same way he was ignoring the fact that he was drenched from the downpour. There was little shelter from the rain to be had from the porch roof. It leaked like a sieve. His gaze went briefly to the ring on her hand and then back to her tense, uncertain features.

"I'm Flint Cottrell." The voice was low, rough, unpolished; the voice of a man who didn't spend a lot of time discussing art films or vintage wine years. "I work here."

That was enough to trigger all of Rani's interior alarms. "The hell you do," she said, and slammed the door in his face. The phone. She would get to the phone and call Mike. If he didn't answer she would know he was on his way. If he did answer, she could tell him to hurry. Rani was slamming the dead bolt in place when something nudged her foot. She jerked back and then glanced down, unnerved and irritated because of it.

"Get out of the way Zipp. There's somebody out there, and he reminds me far too much of you."

The mottled brown tomcat looked up at her with streetwise eyes. He had dashed into temporary hiding when the first knock had sounded on the door. It was his standard routine. Zipp didn't like strangers, especially male strangers. He disappeared and sulked for a long time when people came calling on Rani. This time he hadn't stayed out of sight very long, though, Rani noted distractedly. Here he was already, looking curious. This wasn't part of his normal response.

When the impatient knock sounded again on the door, the huge cat rumbled something that was presumably a question. Rani paid no attention. She turned away, hurrying across the room to where the phone stood on an old pine table. The knock came again as she was dialing Mike Slater's number. Rani's fingers shook slightly as she stood staring at the door, the receiver to her ear. The line was busy.

Rani lowered the instrument slowly into its cradle, her eyes never leaving the door. She was debating with herself about what to do next and seriously wondering whether to slip out through the kitchen, when she saw the dirty white envelope being shoved under the door.

"Read it," the man called through the wooden barrier. "I'd appreciate it if you'd hurry."

Hesitantly Rani moved toward the scruffy envelope. Zipp was already investigating it with interest. "Here, let me see that," Rani murmured, reaching down to pick up the object. She glanced at the front and saw that it was addressed to her. Tearing the envelope open, she reached inside and unfolded the single sheet of paper.

Dear Miss Garroway,
This is to introduce Flint Cottrell. He will be living in the back cottage for a few weeks while doing some yard work around the cottages for us. We were very fortunate to find someone on such short notice this year.

Chagrined, Rani skipped down to the signature at the bottom and read no further. She yanked the dead bolt and flung open the door. The man with the green eyes was still standing where she had left him, his hands shoved into the pockets of his well-worn sheepskin jacket, a stoic, patient expression on his hard face as if he had spent a lot of time waiting around in darkness and rain. The yellowed fleece collar was pulled up around his neck, framing features as weathered as the jacket. Both jacket and man appeared to be nearing forty. It looked as though both had gotten there the hard way.

"I'm terribly sorry, I didn't realize you were going to be my neighbor," Rani said quickly, standing aside. "Please come in. I'm sure you're wet clear through. That porch roof leaks very badly. I doubt that the back cottage is habitable right now. I could have gotten it ready, but no one told me you'd be arriving."

The man said nothing, stepping over the threshold with a kind of aloof arrogance that again made Rani think of her cat. He came to a halt as Zipp moved into his path.

"Don't mind him. That's Zipp. My cat," Rani added helpfully when there was no immediate response. "Short for Zipporo. He usually dashes off to sulk somewhere when visitors arrive, but he seems to find you interesting. Here, let me have your coat. You're soaked."

Flint Cottrell eyed the cat thoughtfully and then slowly began unfastening the old sheepskin jacket. Without a word he handed the garment to Rani. When she took it from him to hang in the hall closet, he ran his broad hand through his damp hair. Droplets of water glistened in the dark-brown depths and then fell to the floor at his feet as Cottrell carelessly scattered them with the movement of his large, blunt fingers.

Automatically Rani followed the descent of the water drops, sighing silently as they hit the wooden floor. Cottrell had apparently used the doormat, but his scuffed boots had still managed to track dampness into the hall. Then she reminded herself that the old hardwood floor had undoubtedly survived far worse disasters.

"Sorry to startle you," Cottrell said, not sounding particularly sorry at all. "Someone should have called. I take it you're Rani Garroway?"

"Yes," Rani agreed crisply. "And someone should definitely have called. Won't you sit down, Mr. Cottrell."

He nodded once, then stalked across the room to take the largest, most comfortable chair in front of the fire. The man apparently didn't need a second invitation. She'd better be careful about what she offered by way of refreshment. He'd probably let her go to the trouble of fixing a five-course dinner if she volunteered. Something about him gave her the impression he made a policy of taking whatever freebies came along in life on the general principle that there probably weren't going to be all that many. He sprawled easily in the chair, watching her as she came slowly toward the fire. Zipp padded toward his feet and nosed curiously around the scarred boots.

Rani glanced down at the letter she still held in her hand. She concentrated on the lines she had skipped over earlier. "You're going to be making some minor repairs on the house and getting the grounds in shape?"

"A sort of general handyman-gardener was how the job was described," Cottrell said calmly. "In return I get free lodging for a few weeks this winter."

From the look of him, the man probably couldn't afford to turn down free lodging. "This is October, Mr. Cottrell. There isn't much to do in a garden in October."

"There's always something to be done in a garden. I'll keep busy. I always earn my keep."

"I'm sure you do." Rani folded the letter very carefully. The light from the fire flickered briefly on her ring, creating a brief illusion of cold green flames trapped in stone as she stuffed the sheet of paper back into its envelope. It was a very fleeting illusion.

The letter had been signed by the people who were renting the main cottage to her. There was one other smaller cottage on the grounds and a great deal of yard that had more or less run wild the past summer from what Rani could see. She didn't know much about gardening, but she suspected the Andersons' garden did need attention. She didn't doubt Mr. Anderson's scrawling signature. "Would you care for a cup of tea, Mr. Cottrell?"

"I'd rather have a shot of whiskey if you've got it. It's cold out there."

Give him an inch, Rani thought humorously. Aloud she said, "I'll see what I can find." She got to her feet and headed toward the kitchen. Behind her Zipp continued staring up into the stranger's face and then, without any warning, leaped onto the wide, overstuffed arm of the chair. Cottrell exchanged a long look with the big cat and then leaned his damp head back against the cushion. He closed his eyes. He didn't appear weary so much as simply determined to rest when the opportunity offered. It was a quality Zipp had.

When Rani emerged from the kitchen with a small glass of golden liquid, her visitor lifted his lashes with the lazy alertness of a dozing feline.

"What's that?"

"Sherry. It's all I've got unless you'd rather have a glass of white wine? The sherry's stronger."

He didn't bother responding to the implied question. Stretching out his arm, he took the delicate glass from her and took a healthy swallow that nearly drained it. His mouth crooked with faint scorn as he tasted the sherry. "This'll do."

Rani flashed him a wry glance as she sank back down into her chair. "You don't know how relieved that makes me feel."

His mouth moved again, this time in a fleeting attempt at a smile. "I didn't mean to be rude. It's been a long drive."

"How long?"

"I left San Francisco over three hours ago. The weather's been like this the whole way. Took me half an hour just to find the Andersons' turnoff after I'd found Reed Lake."

"Perhaps you should have waited and driven up in the morning."

He tilted his head slightly, listening to the faint lecturing tone in her voice. On the arm of the chair Zipp responded in exactly the same fashion, his ears flicking once or twice. The cat knew the tone and generally made a practice of ignoring it.

"I wanted to get here this evening." Flint swallowed the rest of the sherry and closed his eyes again. "That fire feels good. Any heat in the cottage?"

"I don't know. I've never been inside. I'm sure it's got all the amenities or the Andersons wouldn't have told you to use it."

"You never know. I've had people hire me before without bothering to mention the details."

"You're a professional, uh, handyman-gardener?"

He considered that. "Yeah, I guess I am. I suppose you've already eaten dinner?"

Sensing what was coming, Rani wanted to hedge. But her innate honesty got in the way. Even if the honesty hadn't been a problem, the fragrance of the stew simmering on the stove would have been a bit difficult to explain. "No, I haven't, but I was expecting company."

Flint's teeth showed in a strange smile. "And now you've got it. I'm starved."

"You don't understand. A friend of mine is due at any moment and I—" She broke off as the telephone rang imperiously. With a strange twinge of intuition, Rani knew who it was going to be before she picked up the receiver. When Mike Slater spoke on the other end, she wasn't surprised. She knew before he said anything that something had gone wrong. Rani tried to disguise the vague uneasiness she was feeling. If Mike didn't show up this evening, she was going to be left having to deal with Flint Cottrell all on her own. For some reason the prospect wasn't enthralling.

"Hello, Mike. I've been waiting for you."

"Rani, I'm sorry as hell, but there's a tree down across my drive. I won't be able to get the car out until morning. I've been on the phone for the past half hour trying to line up someone to clear the drive, but no one's going to come out on a night like this unless it's an emergency. Mind if I take a rain check on the meal?"

"Of course not, Mike. Everything else okay?"

"Oh, sure. Still got power and the phone's working. How about you?"

Rani looked at the man seated across from her. "I'm all right. I still have power, too. It's turning into quite a storm, isn't it?"

"You can say that again. Listen, keep some candles and a flashlight handy tonight. You might need them. I'd give my eye teeth for some home-cooked stew, but I guess I'll have to wait. I was really looking forward to my first meal with you. Just my luck. Take care. I'll give you a call in the morning."

"Thanks, Mike. I'm very sorry you won't be able to make it tonight. I'll talk to you in the morning." Rani hung up without another word.

Flint watched her face. "I take it there's going to be some extra stew?"

Once again Rani didn't know whether to laugh or groan at Cottrell's blunt approach. "It would appear so, Mr. Cottrell. Would you care for some?"

"Yes." There was a pause. "Please." The "please" sounded rusty. "And call me Flint." He glanced down pointedly at the empty glass in his large hand.

Rani didn't need any more of a hint. "I'll get you some more sherry."

"I'd appreciate it."

"Will you?" Smoothly she took the glass from him and started toward the kitchen. *Or will you simply take it for granted,* she asked silently, *the way stray cats are inclined to do?*

Flint watched her walk into the kitchen, something in him approving the proud, graceful way she moved. He liked the shape of her, he realized. In the snug-fitting jeans and golden-yellow sweater she appeared nicely rounded. There was an appealing hint of lushness in the gentle fullness of her hips and breasts. He had never been attracted to the emaciated-model type.

The rest of her didn't look much like a model, either. Her features were too gentle; very feminine but not sharply defined enough to be riveting, yet they held his full attention when he looked into her face. There was a certain womanly self-confidence in her tawny eyes, but it was a sincere, earnest quality, not cold female arrogance. It was the expression of a woman who had found a place for herself in life, established the boundaries and was satisfied with it. Her hair reminded him of a mixture of dark spices, all deep browns and golds. She wore it in a loose knot on top of her head. From what little he knew of her he guessed she was nearly thirty.

The most important thing was that she had the ring. Flint took a deep breath and flexed his big callused hands. The cat sitting on the chair arm yawned and gave him an inquiring look.

"Don't worry, there's room for both of us," Flint told him quietly. "The legend says so."

"I'm ready to serve," Rani called from the doorway. She watched Zipp jump down from the chair and pad briskly toward her. "You've already had your dinner," she reminded the cat.

"That stew probably smells as good to him as it does to me." Flint came up out of the chair with an easy movement. "Where can I wash my hands?"

Rani nodded toward the hall. "Down there on the right." She turned away to serve the simmering stew and accompanying biscuits. For better or worse she was stuck with uninvited company so she might as well be polite. As she ladled out the aromatic mixture, she started worrying about the condition of the little cottage that sat behind the main house. She was concentrating so intently that she didn't hear Flint walk into the kitchen until he spoke from less than two feet behind her.

"How long are you going to be staying here, Rani?" He took a chair as if he ate at her table every night.

"Three and a half weeks. I arrived a few days ago." She deliberately put a certain amount of repressiveness into her tone. It should have been Mike Slater sitting across from her, not a handyman-gardener who had the arrogance of a free-ranging cat.

"Vacation?"

"Yes. I had some time coming from the library where I work, so I decided I'd better take it or risk losing it." Firmly she turned the conversation around. "What about you, Flint? How long is your job here expected to last?"

"Until I finish a project I'm working on." He slathered butter on one of the biscuits and bit down hungrily. Then he spotted the pot of honey and enthusiastically spooned some onto the remaining portion of biscuit.

"I see." She didn't, of course, but it seemed the logical thing to say under the circumstances. "What made you apply for this particular position?"

He looked up, his emerald eyes trapping hers for an instant. "I didn't exactly apply. I talked my way into the job because I found out you were going to be staying here for a while."

Rani stared at him, her earlier sense of unease turning into an outright chill. Very carefully she put down her fork. "I'm afraid I don't understand."

"It's the ring." He nodded at the green stone set in old metal.

The chill became a faint shivering that she couldn't quite control. Rani's hand closed into a tight fist, and she pushed it into her lap where the ring would be out of sight. "What are you talking about? This ring is junk jewelry. Look, Mr. Cottrell, I don't know what you're up to, but you're starting to make me very nervous. If you've come here to steal my ring, you've made a long trip for nothing. There might be a few dollars in the setting, but the stone itself is practically worthless. Just nicely cut glass. Now, I think you'd better leave."

He ignored her tense command and took another biscuit. "The value of the ring to me lies in the history behind it, not in the stone. Relax, Rani. I'm not here to steal it. It wouldn't do me any good. It doesn't work that way," he added cryptically.

"You're not making any sense."

"I'm writing an article, Rani. In my spare time I do articles on legends and treasures. Objects that have interesting histories like the one behind that ring. A piece on the Clayborne ring is my current project."

"It's just a ring, not a special piece of jewelry," she said bewilderedly. "What about the handyman-gardening job?"

"I told you, it's how I'm going to finance the time to write."

"Have you written a lot of articles, Flint?"

"A few."

She felt as though she were sinking into a bottomless sea. "Have they sold?"

"Some have."

"I don't understand. How did you know about my ring?"

Flint shrugged. "It's one of the legends I've tracked on and off through the years. For some reason I've grown very curious about this particular tale. When I decided to do the article, I tried to find out what had happened to the ring. I discovered it had been left to you by your uncle."

Rani's mouth felt dry. "You seem to know a great deal about me. Far more than I know about you."

"You'll learn."

"About you? I hate to break this to you, Mr. Cottrell, but learning more about you isn't exactly high on my list of priorities."

"You keep a list?" He sounded genuinely interested.

"It was a figure of speech! Just how much do you know about Uncle Ambrose?"

"He was a fine craftsman."

"That's a nice term for it. He made a living creating fake jewelry like this ring. He could make a piece of red glass look like a ruby or cut a bit of crystal so that it shone like a diamond. His work was often good enough to fool anyone but a professional. Supposedly he had an honest business creating paste. There are plenty of people who don't want to wear their genuine valuables in public and prefer to have duplicates made. But the truth of the matter is that my uncle made his real money working with jewel thieves who wanted to leave a piece of paste behind when they stole the real thing. My uncle's stuff was so good that often the switch wasn't discovered for years."

"You seem to know a fair amount about Ambrose's career," Flint said mildly as he started energetically on the stew.

Rani's mouth curved wryly. "I learned it the awkward way along with the rest of my family after Uncle Ambrose was killed in a car accident back East a couple of months ago. When his business accounts were examined after the funeral, a great deal of information came to light. Uncle Ambrose kept excellent books. Two sets of them. Several old jewel theft cases were partially cleared up, thanks to Uncle Ambrose's accounts.

"And after his death you inherited that ring."

"Along with a whole bunch of other fake jewelry. My uncle's work is actually quite beautiful. The jewelry was forwarded to me by his lawyer, who said Ambrose wanted me to have it. I'm not sure why. It's not as if we were close. Ambrose kept his distance from the rest of the family. We never saw much of him through the years." Rani pulled her hand out of her lap and deliberately spread her fingers so that the kitchen light reflected off the emerald-green ring. "But it's all equally false, Flint. Believe me."

"You're an expert?"

"No. I had them appraised. Some are plain glass, beautifully cut. Others are inferior stones cut and polished so perfectly they look like the real thing. The settings look good, just as this one does. But they're not worth more than any other piece of nice costume jewelry."

Flint eyed the ring thoughtfully. "You seem to enjoy wearing that ring."

Rani waggled her fingers. "I like all the pieces. They're fun to wear. Very pretty in their own way. Big, gaudy pieces of colorful junk. I've always liked bright colors." She flushed in a burst of self-deprecating amusement and glanced down at her bright sweater. "I have rather garish tastes, you see."

"Is that right?" There was a flicker of humor in the green eyes.

"Believe me, if this thing was real, I'd have it sitting in a safe-deposit box," Rani stated firmly. "I wouldn't dare wear it."

"I've just told you that the value of the ring lies in the story behind it."

"Any legend worth its salt would be about a real emerald, not a phony one. If there ever was a genuine stone in this ring, Uncle Ambrose removed it long ago. If the police are to be believed about Uncle Ambrose's business methods, it would have been cut up and sold on the black market." Rani picked up her spoon and began attacking her bowl of stew with a grim determination. She could only hope she'd said enough to discourage Cottrell if he was here with some vague notion of stealing her ring. It would be impossible to physically kick him out of the house. The man was big. But surely he wouldn't be sitting here chatting calmly about the ring if he intended to steal it.

"Legends are strange things. Very persistent things. Aren't you even curious about the ones concerning your ring?"

"Not particularly."

"Suit yourself. Is there any more stew?"

Rani stifled a sigh. "Yes, there's more stew. Have you brought linens and dishes with you, Flint?" She got to her feet to ladle out more food. "I doubt the cottage has any. From what I've seen of the place it's been vacant quite a while."

"I'll get by. I've slept in worse places."

"I'll bet," Rani muttered as she brought the dish back to the table. "When you've finished eating, I'll show you the cottage."

He looked up at her searchingly. "You're anxious to get rid of me, aren't you?"

"I'm sorry if I appear rude, but, frankly, this evening isn't going the way I planned, at all."

"Because I'm not the man you spoke to on the phone?"

"That's certainly part of the reason," she replied too sweetly. Rani resumed her seat. "The other part is that it makes me extremely nervous to know you've followed me all this way just because of a fake ring."

Flint put down his spoon and touched her hand, his gaze intent. "Don't be nervous. I brought good references, haven't I?"

"That letter from the Andersons? I don't know if it's a good reference or not." She withdrew her fingers, instinctively retreating from his touch.

"It's legitimate." He sounded arrogantly offended, as if he weren't accustomed to having his word questioned.

"Oh, I'm not doubting the signature. But who knows how much they knew about you when they rented the cottage to you? Who knows what you told them to get the job? You admitted you talked them into thinking they needed a . . . a handyman-gardener."

"Suspicious little thing, aren't you?"

"Wouldn't you be if you were in my shoes?" Rani asked coolly.

To her surprise he appeared to give the matter serious consideration. "I don't know. I can't imagine what it would be like to be in your shoes. I can imagine being attracted to you, but I can't imagine being you. We're at opposite ends of a spectrum."

Rani set down her spoon, aware that her pulse was racing for no good reason. No, she immediately told herself, that wasn't true. Fear was a good reason. "I think it's time I showed you to the cottage, Flint."

He stared at her for a moment, taking in the sudden, regal tilt of her chin and the firm decision in her eyes. Then, to Rani's infinite relief, he nodded. "All right." He reached for one last biscuit, put down his napkin and got to his feet.

Rani didn't hesitate. She wanted him out of the house, and he appeared to be in a mood to go. She didn't dare waste the opportunity. "I'll get a flashlight."

"I have to get some things from the jeep." Flint swallowed the last of his biscuit and started toward the front door, pausing to pull his old sheepskin jacket out of the closet. Bareheaded, he stepped out into the rain, closing the door behind him. Zipp lifted his head to watch him go and then went back to dozing in front of the fire.

Rani scurried around, putting on a yellow trench coat and locating her red umbrella. She wanted to meet Flint outside so that he wouldn't have any further excuse for coming back into the house. When she yanked open the front door, he was already standing there, waiting for her. He had a scarred leather travel bag slung over one shoulder.

Rani felt a flash of guilt as she realized he was already wet again. "Here, get under the umbrella," she instructed briskly, opening it. Obediently he ducked beneath the shield. She had to stretch her arm high in order to cover him. It was awkward. "Do you have a key?"

"The Andersons gave me one."

"Fine. The cottage is around back. This way." Rani led him around the corner of the old mountain house, following a brick path that was missing several bricks. "Watch your step," she called above the steady drone of the rain.

She promptly stepped into one of the small holes in the path, herself. "Damn!"

Flint took her arm in a grip that resembled a predator's hold on its prey. "Are you all right?"

"Yes, yes, I'm fine, thank you." Unobtrusively she attempted to free her arm. He didn't appear to notice her efforts.

"I'll make sure I take care of this path first thing," he said seriously.

Rani gritted her teeth. "Wonderful."

The cottage loomed up out of the wet darkness, uninviting and depressing. When Flint shoved his key into the lock, the door swung open to reveal a room of deepest gloom. Fortunately the light switch worked. Unfortunately it didn't do much for the general sense of neglect and disrepair. There wasn't much to the old cottage, just a main room that served as both a sitting and sleeping area, a fireplace, bath and a tiny alcove of a kitchen with a small assortment of aging appliances. Rani began to feel guilty again, even though she knew she had absolutely no reason for it. Still, she couldn't imagine anyone not being depressed about the idea of living there for a few weeks.

"You may want to change your mind about the arrangement you made with the Andersons," she said, glancing around the room.

"I doubt it." Flint dropped his leather bag onto the old linoleum floor. "I've learned to take what I can get. This place is free, remember? Can't beat a deal like that."

Irritation began to build in Rani. "You could if you had a decent job. You'd be able to afford something much better than this. Have you spent your whole life bouncing around from one makeshift job to another?"

He slanted her an unfathomable glance. "That and chasing legends."

"Oh, yes. I forgot about the legends," she retorted tightly.

"You shouldn't. Especially now that you've become part of one." Flint's tone was suddenly very soft, faintly dangerous.

"If you're talking about the ring—" she began resolutely.

"I am," he assured her.

"Then you can just forget this particular legend!"

"I can't do that. It's the basis of my next magazine article, remember? Besides," he added with a fleeting smile, "if there's any truth to the legend, I can't forget about it."

"What are you talking about?"

"Maybe if I tell you the first part of the tale, you'll understand."

"I told you, I'm not interested," she tried to say. But she was. Vitally interested. Flint seemed to sense it.

"The story goes back to the seventeen hundreds," Flint said as he closed the door behind her. "I'll spare you the details, since you say you're not interested, but the important part is that the woman who owns the ring has an affinity for cats and a woman's power over one particular man. She doesn't know who he is, but once he's drawn to her his future, as well as her own, is sealed."

"That sounds very uncomfortable."

"In each generation that the ring finds its way onto the hand of a woman who can control it, there's a man who is fated to be drawn into her power."

"Whoever said life was fair?" Rani smiled with a flippancy she didn't really feel. "Lucky for you, this ring is a fake."

"I don't know about that. I seem to be here, don't I?"

Rani stepped back, her hand on the doorknob. "Does the legend say what happens to men who chase false rings?"

Flint shook his head, watching as she opened the door and prepared to flee back to the main house. "No. But the second part of the tale explains the technique the ensnared man uses to make certain the lady is as bound to him as he is to her."

"Really?" she asked scornfully. "What's he supposed to do? Boil up a caldron full of dead bat's tongues?"

"Nothing that complicated," Flint said gently. "All he has to do is take the lady to bed. After that the lady belongs to him, body and soul."

Rani's breath seemed to catch in her throat. Her body was suddenly vibrating with the primitive need to run, even though Flint hadn't taken a step toward her. It was all she could do to summon a cool, derisive expression. "Lucky for both of us then that the ring is a fake. Good night, Flint."

"I'll see you back to the house."

"No," she said with soft arrogance, "you won't." She stepped out into the rain and slammed the door behind her.

It wasn't until she reached the kitchen door of the main house and stood shaking out the umbrella under the leaking porch roof that she realized she'd been followed. Startled, she glanced up and peered through the rain-swept darkness. Flint was standing there, not more than a few feet behind her, his hands deep in the pockets of his jacket as he watched her.

"Good night, Rani."

She couldn't think of anything to say so she hurried inside and locked her door. Leaning back against the wood, her hands on the knob, she drew several steadying breaths and then lifted her lashes to stare at the empty bowls of stew on the table. Zipp was calmly preparing to help himself to what remained in Rani's dish.

"Get off that table, Zipp!"

Unrepentant, Zipp jumped down and wandered back out into the living room. Thoroughly annoyed, Rani scooped up the dishes and carried them over to the sink. The cat and Flint had a similar philosophy of life apparently. They both took what they could get.

She was going to have to keep an eye on both of them, Rani told herself as she did the dishes. She was going to have to stay in control. The life she had created for herself was very safe, very risk-free. She had no intention of changing her pattern of living to accommodate a man who had eyes that held green fire in their depths.

Two

―――

The first thing Rani noticed the next morning was that the storm had passed through, leaving a chilled, slightly damp but basically sunny day in its wake. The second thing she noticed was that she didn't appear to be alone in the house. The distinct clash and clang of pots and pans and a slamming refrigerator door came from the kitchen.

She could probably assume it wasn't a burglar, Rani decided as she shoved back the covers and padded over to the closet. Most burglars would have better manners. She wrapped the turquoise-and-shocking-pink bathrobe around herself, stepped into her fluffy bright pink slippers and started grimly down the hall.

At the entrance to the kitchen she came to a halt, silently studying the scene before her. Zipp was seated on the windowsill, watching with interest as Flint systematically created chaos. Cottrell was working hard at the project. A wide assortment of utensils and bowls dotted the countertop. Two frying pans had been set out on the stove. A carton of milk stood open, and the lids were off the canisters that lined one wall. Flint himself was standing in front of the open refrigerator, examining its contents as if he were plotting an assault strategy. He was dressed for attack in an olive-drab fatigue sweater and a pair of jeans. Like the jacket he had worn last night, both garments looked as if they'd been around a long while. The income of an itinerant handyman-gardener was probably rather meager.

Rani propped one hand against the doorjamb and drummed her fingers meaningfully. "If you'll give me a minute, I'll find you an apron."

Flint didn't glance up from his serious perusal of the refrigerator's interior. "That's okay. I don't need one."

"Are you sure?" she asked dryly. "You appear to be about to cook breakfast for a battalion."

He looked around when she said that, his green eyes moving with interest over her bright robe and sleep-tousled hair. "No. Just you and me and the cat."

"Really? I'm included? To what do I owe the honor?"

"I got the refrigerator going but there isn't any food in the other cottage," he explained simply, still looking at her. "I felt like pancakes."

The intentness of his stare was beginning to ruffle her composure. Rani resisted the urge to clutch the lapels of her robe more tightly closed. She was decently covered. There was no reason to let him unnerve her. "I see. So you just decided you'd break into my kitchen and make yourself a batch?"

"I haven't had pancakes for a long time."

"That's certainly a valid explanation for all this." She waved a hand at the clutter on the countertop.

"I just felt like pancakes," he repeated stubbornly.

"Do you make a habit of invading other people's homes when you feel like helping yourself to something they have?"

Flint closed the refrigerator door and leaned against it, his arms folded across his chest. "This house and the cottage seemed to be part of the same package rental. I sort of think of it as all one territory. After all, I'm going to be working on both as well as the garden."

Rani straightened away from the wall, no longer making any pretence of controlling her irritation. Her normally well-ordered life did not allow for this sort of disturbance. "I think we should get something clear between us, Flint. You are installed in the small cottage. I am renting this house. You will enter my portion of the 'territory' only upon invitation. We are not all one big happy family vacationing under the same roof. If I remember that letter from the Andersons, you are the hired help. Nothing more. Do you understand the situation now?"

He watched her through slightly narrowed eyes. "I understand," Flint said softly. "I just felt like having pancakes. I told you, there isn't any food in the cottage."

Rani gritted her teeth and waved one hand in a gesture of frustrated disgust. "All right! You can have your pancakes. But this is my kitchen and I will make them. You will kindly get the hell out of here until I call you for breakfast. Go pluck weeds or something."

Flint ran a hand around the back of his neck. "What I'd really like is a shower. The one in the cottage wasn't working."

Rani glared at him, appalled at the new direction of the conversation. "Not my bathroom! You're surely not suggesting that you have access to my bathroom."

"Just the shower. The rest of the plumbing in the cottage works fine."

"I don't believe this."

"Don't worry, I won't use all the hot water."

"I'm not taking my chances." She whirled and stalked back down the hall. "I'll take my shower first. You can have whatever hot water is left over. In the meantime, don't touch another thing in that kitchen."

"Yes, ma'am."

Rani groaned inwardly at the suspiciously meek tone of his voice, then gathered a pair of jeans and a crimson-and-papaya colored pullover and stepped into the bathroom. She locked the door firmly behind her. The action made her wonder how Flint had gotten into the kitchen. She could have sworn she'd locked the door the night before when she'd returned from the cottage. Then she remembered her sense of nervous awareness when she'd glanced out into the rainy darkness and realized he'd followed her. Maybe she'd been too startled to remember to lock the kitchen door. Or maybe he was good at getting into locked places.

Half an hour later she poured pancake batter into neat circles on the heated griddle and laconically wondered how on earth she'd let herself get maneuvered into making breakfast for Flint Cottrell.

"This has gone far enough, Zipp," she confided to the cat who was sunning himself in the window. "I've got to get control of the situation or the next few weeks are going to be a disaster."

Down the hall the shower finally clicked off. Flint sauntered into the kitchen a few minutes later, running a rather beat-up comb through his damp hair.

"Smells good. Hey, you've got real maple syrup, not brown sugar water."

He wore such an air of pleased expectation on his hard face as he sat down at the table that Rani almost felt guilty about the grudging way she was fixing breakfast. Almost.

Her natural wariness about the bizarre situation in which she found herself was enough to prevent an outright attack of feminine guilt.

"You can pick up some supplies in Reed Lake today so that you'll be able to cook your own breakfast tomorrow morning," Rani said as she placed a stack of steaming pancakes in front of him. "Also your own dinner this evening," she added bluntly.

He nodded disinterestedly, his attention clearly on the pancakes as he carefully buttered each one and poured syrup over the top. "This is nice country. Clean and green. I noticed you could see the lake from your living room window. Can't see anything from my cottage except the trees."

"Theoretically gardeners should be more interested in the greenery than the lake."

"I guess."

"Have you done a lot of gardening, Flint?"

"When the jobs come up, I take them."

"But you've worked quite a bit as a handyman also?" Rani pressed as she seated herself.

"Yeah."

"Have you, uh, had any other professions?" She wasn't sure why she was asking the questions. A strange kind of perverse curiosity probably.

He looked up. "I've been fairly flexible. I've generally done whatever came along. I like gardening best, though."

"Your résumé must be quite long by now," Rani observed with a hint of disapproval.

"It probably would be if I ever got around to typing one. Most of the people I've worked for didn't expect to see formal résumés."

"How long have you been job-hopping like this?"

Flint shrugged. "Since I got out of school. I took a job on a freighter during my junior year in college. One thing led to another. I never looked back. Tended bar for a while in Singapore. Acted as a stringer for one of the wire services in North Africa. Worked in the oil fields in the Middle East. Did a stint as a guide for some anthropologists in Indonesia. Hired myself out as a bodyguard for an industrialist in Italy. The industrialist had a great garden. I spent a lot of time in it when I was off duty. There's always something for a man who's flexible and who doesn't mind hard work."

Rani's fork went still. "And in between you chase legends."

"I like tracking them down," he admitted.

"What do you do with them when you track them down?"

"Find out the real truth, do an article and try to sell it."

"The real truth?" Rani paused. "What sort of article are you planning to do on the Clayborne ring, Flint?"

"A factual one. I'm going to straighten out the record on it the way I've done with the other legends I've chased."

"What do you mean?"

"I prove the wild tales are generally false."

"You mean show that things such as the Bermuda Triangle aren't really mysterious or strange after all? That there's no curse on the mummy of a certain Egyptian pharaoh? That everything can be explained in a rational fashion? That sort of approach?"

He nodded, pouring more syrup on his pancakes. "You've got it."

Rani straightened in her chair, frowning across the table. "I've got news for you, Flint. You're doomed before you start. Take my word for it. I work in a public library and I know what people read. They don't want their legends debunked. You'd do better to write articles emphasizing the exotic nature of the legends, not the truth. I have a fairly good feel for what people are interested in and most of them want the wonder and the mystery left in their legends.''

Flint gave her an impatient glance. ''Well, I write the truth.''

''Had it occurred to you they may not want to read it?'' Suddenly Rani held up her hand. ''Forget I said anything. Why on earth am I sitting here arguing with you about it? You're certainly entitled to write anything you please. In fact, it sounds as if you've spent most of your life doing exactly as you please. You're obviously not going to listen to someone like me.''

''Why do you say that?'' He sounded genuinely interested.

''Well, it's pretty clear you've indulged yourself to the hilt in the classic male fantasy of never being tied down. There's no reason on earth why you should start listening to someone trying to tell you to do something you don't feel like doing. What's the longest period of time you've ever stayed on any one job?''

''I don't know. A year or so maybe. No, wait, there were at least two years in Indonesia.''

''I won't ask if you've ever been married,'' Rani murmured, finishing her pancakes.

Flint's brows came together in a hard line. Beneath them his green eyes were brooding and watchful. ''There's never been the time nor the place nor the woman.''

''Bull. You mean you've never wanted to make a commitment that would require you to give up your freedom.'' She gazed at him very levelly. ''Do you want any more pancakes?''

''Wait a minute. What do you mean with that crack about commitments?''

"Most men aren't terribly good at making them and keeping them," she explained, as if he were a little slow in the head. "Not long-term ones. Ask any woman."

"I'm asking you."

"Oh, I'm a great witness. My father came and went all during my childhood until one day when I was about fourteen he announced he couldn't handle being a husband and a father any longer. He had his own life to think of and he didn't want to waste it on a nine-to-five job in the suburbs and a dull little family. He divorced Mom and walked out for good. Went off to live his dreams, I expect. Since getting out of college I've discovered that the world is full of men who can't make commitments. At least not to a woman. Most of them would probably secretly sell their souls to live your type of life-style, though. Do you want any more pancakes or not?"

"You seem to have accepted this particular weakness you've identified in the male of the species," Flint growled, ignoring her question about the pancakes.

"I have. I've just recently turned thirty. What's the sense of growing older if you don't also grow up?"

"What do you do? Go through life being wonderfully understanding and not making any demands on the men you go to bed with?" he demanded roughly.

Rani blinked owlishly, uncertain of his mood now. "Men can be quite entertaining on occasion. Some have a great sense of humor. Some are talented. Some are even quite intelligent. I enjoy their company at times. But I've learned that it's best not to let them get too close. Physically or emotionally. The thing with men is not to take them too seriously." she explained gently.

"Are you sleeping with that guy who called last night?"

She stiffened. "Mike Slater? That's really none of your business, is it?"

"I keep forgetting. I'm just the hired help, aren't I?"

"I'll try to make sure you remember in the future." Angrily Rani got to her feet and picked up her dishes. The sunlight streaming through the window glinted off the green stone in her ring as she dumped the leftover pancake batter into the garbage.

"Wait a second," Flint yelped as the batter disappeared into an empty can, "I was going to have some more."

"I gave you your chance," she reminded him with a sense of satisfaction. "You didn't answer my question when I asked if you wanted more. So you're out of luck."

"You run a tight ship," Flint complained as he grudgingly brought his own dishes over to the sink.

Rani turned to confront him, her hands braced on the sink behind her. "I'm glad you realize that. For a while there this morning I was afraid I'd have to spell it out more clearly. This is my home for the next few weeks, Flint. I run it my way. Stray cats who happen to wander in and out when it pleases them will have to accept that or stay the hell out of here."

His mouth curved faintly, and he glanced at Zipp. "Is that how you see me? A stray cat who just happened to wander over the threshold last night?"

"The analogy seemed appropriate."

"Yeah," he said thoughtfully. "It does. But I don't think you realize yet just how appropriate." He reached out to touch her ring. Rani jumped a little as his callused fingers drifted over the back of her hand. "The lady who commands the ring attracts stray cats. You're the current owner of the ring and therefore only you can wield its power. You can have as many cats under your spell as you wish, but there's only one man in your future, Rani."

She shivered a little in spite of herself, but her voice was steady. "What a pity. You mean I only get to exercise my power over one man?"

"And a few stray cats such as Zipp."

"Do I get to pick the man and the cats?"

"No. They pick you. Didn't you know that, Rani? When it comes time to settle down, free-roaming alley cats always choose their own homes. A man who's spent his whole life roaming does the same."

She swallowed at the sight of the subtle green fire in his eyes. "I thought you said that it was one particular man's fate to be summoned to the lady who wears the ring, to be in her power."

"Sometimes it's hard to tell the difference between fate and an act of will."

He seemed to move closer. Rani could still feel his fingers lightly gliding over the back of her hand. She was suddenly, vitally, intensely aware of him, and the knowledge was frightening. She felt trapped against the sink, far to conscious of the sleek power in his body and the sense of urgency she discovered in herself.

"I know all about acts of will," she managed.

"Do you?"

"I'm going to exercise one right now. Get out of my kitchen and get to work, Flint Cottrell. You were hired to pull weeds and fix broken footpaths. When you're done with that, I'll make out a list of other things that need attention around here, starting with your shower. Now move! Breakfast is over."

He stared down at her for a long moment, reading the determination in her face. For a few timeless seconds a subtle battle of wills was waged. Rani felt it in every inch of her body. She refused to back down. Instinct warned her that retreat would only be inviting some unspecified disaster. She didn't dare back down or turn the small scene into a joke. She was completely serious, and she knew Flint realized it. Without any warning, he appeared to accept the situation.

"Yes, ma'am. I'll get to work right away. Thanks for the pancakes. Like I said, it's been a long time." He turned and walked out of the kitchen. A moment later the door slammed shut behind him.

Rani realized she had forgotten to breathe for a couple of tense moments. She inhaled deeply, staring at the closed door. Then, very slowly, she swung around to draw water into the sink. The pleasantly ugly cat on the windowsill cocked one ear inquiringly.

"I think I won that round, Zipp. It was close, but I did win it. The trick will be to stay on top. Give that man an inch and I can forget all about the mile. He'll take it before I even realize what's happening."

Zipp yawned and stretched out one paw to bat playfully at the dishrag.

"I'm not sure you're on my side, Zipp."

Two hours later Flint paused to lean on his rake and watch as the somewhat staid-looking Oldsmobile nosed out of the driveway and onto the main road that circled the water. Rani's car appeared to have been purchased with an eye for safety and utility. Flint guessed she was the type who never took chances when she drove and who wouldn't dream of buying herself a hot little sports car. He was coming to the conclusion that her vividly colored clothes constituted her chief outlet for the adventurous impulses that cropped up in her mind. She was a lady who didn't take undue risks.

Rani was on her way to Reed Lake, the small town located at the north end of the large, meandering lake. She was going to do a little shopping and pick up her mail, she'd explained as she'd waved the keys at him on her way out to the car.

Flint knew she was going to do more than that. He'd heard the phone ring in the living room earlier when he'd been working at the front of the house, and his intuition told him that the man who hadn't made it to dinner the night before had probably called to set up a lunch date in town. Flint wondered if she'd tell Mike Slater about her substitute guest. There was also the possibility she might not take Flint's presence seriously enough to bother explaining his presence to another man.

Flint's fingers locked fiercely around the rake handle, and he went back to cleaning leaves out of the hedge. Quite suddenly nothing on earth was more important than having Rani Garroway take him seriously.

He hadn't missed the amused disdain in her eyes that morning when she'd casually implied he shared a commitment problem with the rest of his sex. She seemed to think his past was ample evidence to support the implication. What really bothered him now was that he hadn't viewed his wandering life as a result of an inability to settle down or make a commitment. He knew it looked that way to other people, but it hadn't felt that way to him.

Rani didn't understand, Flint told himself. She didn't know what it felt like to be driven all of your adult life by a restlessness that didn't allow any peace. She couldn't know the feelings of isolation and aloneness it brought, that sense of being completely on your own. After a while the knowledge that a man could depend on no one but himself became so much a part of him that he stopped trying to imagine any other way of living. He kept going; kept searching for something he couldn't name because he didn't seem to have any choice.

Flint knew it wasn't a sense of wanderlust that had kept him on the move since his early twenties. It was something far more insidious and potentially destructive. It had to do with an odd kind of desperation, a feeling that out *there*, somewhere, lay the answers he was seeking, the end of his quest.

It was strange. For a long time he hadn't consciously thought about the unnamed demons that drove him. Years ago he'd stopped trying to analyze and fight them. He'd come to accept them as a part of himself. He'd kept searching, even though he frankly admitted he didn't really know what he sought. Chasing legends became a way of chasing an elusive truth about himself.

But last night when Rani had opened her door to him, everything had begun to change. It was as if his very isolated, very private world had shifted subtly on its axis. He'd crossed the threshold, had sat down in front of Rani's fire and had realized that things that had never been in focus for him were suddenly beginning to solidify.

That morning he'd awakened with an overpowering hunger for pancakes. The chilled autumn morning, together with the tall, sunlit pines and peaceful lake, had demanded a breakfast of hot pancakes and real maple syrup. Flint hadn't quite understood it. Usually he could take or leave a pancake breakfast the way he could take or leave anyone or anything. But that morning he'd needed it. Memories of teenage camping trips, Sunday morning breakfast as a child and the occasional times in his past when things had seemed to be going right all coalesced into a desire for pancakes. Hot, homemade pancakes fitted the morning perfectly. He'd known without asking that Rani's kitchen would contain the makings.

He hadn't realized until he was blundering around between cupboards, refrigerator and too many pots and pans that he needed more than pancakes. He needed someone there to share them. The sense of things coming slowly into focus had intensified when Rani had walked into the kitchen and made breakfast for him.

The problem was that Rani hadn't seemed to realize how right the whole situation was, or perhaps something in her was afraid of seeing the rightness of it. He'd known at once that she was careful and cautious by nature and that she didn't approve of people who weren't. She'd sat across the table, delicately lecturing and scolding and dismissing him until he'd suddenly wanted to pull her down onto the kitchen floor and make love to her until she acknowledged his right to be there.

He'd known just how he'd do it, too, even though the wild impulse had startled him. He would have kissed her until the feminine challenge in her tawny eyes was replaced with passion. Then he would have held her very close, crushing her soft breasts against his chest while he stripped away the brightly colored sweater and the snug jeans. Flint knew with sure instinct that her body would fit his perfectly. He could imagine the soft roundness of her thighs, the heat he would generate in her and the clinging, yielding way she would hold him.

He would have made love to her until she took him very, very seriously; until she admitted he had a right to make love to her.

Instead he'd let her order him out of the kitchen and send him off to work. Flint swore softly and wielded the rake with controlled force. He reminded himself grimly that if the legend of the Clayborne ring held any truth at all, the scene in the kitchen had ended the only way it could for now. After all, the lady wore the ring. Until he'd taken her to bed, he was more or less at her mercy.

When he was near Rani he had to keep reminding himself that he didn't believe in legends.

Rani ordered a hamburger with an extra-large portion of
french fries and sat back as Mike Slater told his amusing tale
of trying to get the fallen tree cleared out of the drive of the
lakefront cottage he was renting. Beyond the café window
the main street of Reed Lake was busier than usual as trucks
full of deer hunters stopped at the gas station, bought beer
from the general store or stopped at one of the two cafés for
coffee.

Rani frowned at the sight of the rifles hanging in the back
of the red Ford pickup that was parked just outside the
window. Two laughing men in camouflage shirts were returning from the grocery store with six-packs of beer under
their arms.

"Why the disapproving librarian look?" Mike asked
good-naturedly, following her gaze.

Rani smiled wryly. "You'd think those men would have
better sense than to mix rifles and beer."

Mike grinned, his pleasantly intense eyes crinkling at the
corners. "Are you kidding? The main reason they're here is
to have an excuse to party all night long with their good
buddies. For most of them this is their yearly fling away
from the wife and the kids. For two week each year they get
to pretend they're macho survivalists instead of nine-to-five
clock-watchers. The deer hunting just provides the excuse.
If it's any consolation, you can bet most of them won't
manage to kill a damn thing."

"I trust that will be some consolation to the deer. I suppose hunting is an example of the old male bonding thing.
It's one way men prove their manhood to themselves."

"And have a good time while they're doing it. Don't be too hard on them, Rani. The tradition of hunting season is too old and established for you to be able to change it."

Rani was forced to laugh a little. "I know. I wouldn't think of depriving men of their yearly flings. But I'm glad you're not a hunter, Mike."

He leaned back in the booth and smiled at her. "If I were, would you be having lunch with me?"

She shook her head. "I doubt it. I much prefer artists."

"Actually, a real macho hunter with a pickup under him could probably have managed that tree in my driveway a lot more efficiently than I did." Mike chuckled as he continued with his story. His blue eyes were full of self-directed amusement.

Rani sat across from him and realized she was mentally comparing Mike to Flint Cottrell. But how could you compare a successful artist to an alley cat? Mike was in his mid-thirties, his features sharp and aquiline, his sandy-brown hair a little long and a bit on the shaggy side, which only seemed appropriate for his profession. He had a lean, wiry build, and there was a certain artistic intensity about him that fit the image of a painter. He wore a long-sleeved, white, open-necked shirt and a pair of faded, paint-stained jeans. He had a pair of expensive running shoes on his feet. Rani had met him the first day she'd stopped at the Reed Lake post office to pick up her general delivery mail.

As in most small towns, the post office was a cheerful meeting place for the regulars as well as visitors. It was also the center of local gossip, and Mrs. Hobson, the woman in charge of the Reed Lake post office, took her role as good-natured gossipmonger seriously. She was already waiting with avid attention to see if anything serious developed between the vacationing librarian and the wintering artist.

A casual friendship between Rani and Mike had sprung up immediately, and Rani had a hunch that if she allowed it to develop further, Mike would be more than willing. But Rani had no intention of getting too involved with an artist or a vacation romance. It wasn't the sort of thing she did. She knew where to draw the line to ensure that her safe little world stayed neat and orderly. As she bit into her overstuffed hamburger, Rani remembered Flint asking bluntly if she was sleeping with Mike. Nothing could have been farther from the truth.

"How about another try at dinner?" Mike asked, pouring ketchup on his french fries. "My treat this time. I haven't got the nerve to ask you to go to the trouble of fixing another meal after I failed to show up for the last one. There's that resort restaurant at the other end of town. The one that overlooks the lake. We could give it a try."

"Sounds great. Tomorrow evening?"

He nodded. "I'll make reservations. With all these hunters in town, we might need them."

"I doubt it. This crowd doesn't look like it dresses for dinner. These guys will be sticking to taverns and cafés, not dining at a resort. I'll be ready at six. Okay?"

"I'll clean the paint off my hands in honor of the occasion," Mike assured her.

Rani parked the Oldsmobile in the driveway of her rented house an hour later, shoved open the door and reached behind the driver's seat to pick up an armful of groceries. She was bent over, struggling with the heavy bag, when she felt a large, masculine hand settle all too casually on the small of her back, just above the waistband of her jeans.

She overreacted, her instincts telling her at once whose hand it was. "What the...? Flint!" Her head came up too quickly, striking the roof of the car. "Ouch!"

"Are you all right?" There was genuine concern in his voice. "Here, I'll take that bag for you."

She backed hurriedly out of the way and collided with his sweat-streaked, bare chest. The fatigue sweater had apparently been long since discarded. When she glanced upward, she saw the rivulets of perspiration gathering at a point just beneath the line of his throat and trickling down through crisp, dark hair. He frowned at her as she ducked aside and then he leaned forward to pick up the bag. She wasn't really sure she wanted to know how he had received the wicked-looking old scar on his shoulder.

"Is your head okay?" Flint demanded as he straightened with the bag cradled easily in one arm. Zipp, as usual, had raced out to meet Rani and was now making himself a nuisance around her feet.

"It's fine, thank you. Just fine," she declared firmly. "Get out of my way, Zipp. Here, I can manage the bag, Flint."

"That's all right. I'll take it into the kitchen for you. How was lunch?"

"How did you know I had lunch? Have I got ketchup on my sweater or something?"

Flint shook his head, leading the way toward the front door. "I just figured you were probably meeting that guy for lunch. The one who didn't show last night."

"What amazing perception. As it happens, I'm meeting him for dinner tomorrow night, too." Rani shoved her key into the front door lock with undue energy. "Anything else you'd like to know about my schedule?"

"What are you doing for dinner tonight?"

"Dining alone," she informed him with a sugary smile. She knew what was coming and vowed silently not to let it happen. She had to put her foot down somewhere. The problem was that once you'd fed a stray cat it was damned tough to get rid of him. She should never have fed Flint Cottrell the night before.

Flint looked at the black four-wheel drive Jeep he'd arrived in the previous evening and then back down into Rani's wary eyes. "I don't think I'm going to get a chance to drive into town this afternoon. There's a lot of work around here. I won't be able to pick up any supplies."

"Really? How lucky for you that I took the liberty of picking up a few things for you."

A startled expression flashed through his eyes. "You did?"

"Uh-huh. Milk and cereal for your breakfast tomorrow morning and a frozen dinner you can pop into the oven this evening. I also picked up a six-pack of beer for you." At the time she'd selected the items in Reed Lake's small grocery store she'd been pleased with herself for keeping one step ahead of Flint. Now Rani found herself having to stifle a niggling sense of guilt.

"A TV dinner?" he asked reproachfully as he followed her into the kitchen. "You bought me a TV dinner?"

"Don't worry. From the sound of things you've been out of the country a lot during the past few years so you probably don't realize how they've changed. They're much better than they used to be. I got you fettuccine Alfredo."

"I don't go in for fancy gourmet stuff," he stated, setting the bag down on the kitchen counter with an air of challenge.

"Think of it as macaroni and cheese."

He swung around, suddenly filling her kitchen with dark, lean, male aggression. It was an aggression made all the more intimidating by his obvious self-control. "I'd rather have whatever you're having."

Rani swallowed and stood firm. "I'm afraid that's not possible. I'm eating alone tonight, Flint. Hadn't you better get back to work? I wouldn't want to keep you from your chores.''

She had the distinct impression it was touch and go for a moment. Flint looked as if he were having difficulty deciding how far to push her. Then, just when she was very much afraid he was going to carry the challenge further, he picked up the six-pack of beer, and turned and stalked to the door.

Rani sank into a chair, relief overcoming her for a moment. The situation was getting outrageous. She was right to take a firm stand. She had to draw the line and make it stick because if she didn't Flint Cottrell would just keep pushing.

She had no intention of letting a man with Flint's unstable background push his way into her world.

Three

Rani didn't know what woke her shortly before midnight. She had read until nearly eleven and had been asleep for less than an hour. There was no sense of danger, merely a feeling of something being different in the room. She lay still for a few minutes, analyzing the situation with sleepy care. Then she turned slowly on her side to peer at the curtained window. The shadowed figure of a man stood outside the glass, his solid shoulders silhouetted in the watery moonlight.

When she realized there was someone in the garden, Rani's sense of danger came belatedly into play. The quick breath she sucked in caught in her throat, and her hands suddenly tingled with that prickly feeling she always got when she was startled or alarmed. For an instant she couldn't move. With a sense of horror, she recalled that the catch on the window was broken, and there was no way to lock it.

But even as she watched, her nerves chilling, the figure slipped past the window. There was a soft, rumbling meow and a small thump as Zipp uncoiled from the foot of the bed and leaped onto the sill. The cat poked his head between the thin, white cotton curtains and sat staring steadily into the darkness.

Rani suddenly knew who was abroad in the garden. What she couldn't figure out was why Flint was roaming outside at this late hour. It was cold, probably no more than thirty-five or forty degrees outside. The days had fallen into the typical pattern of autumn in the mountains: chilled nights and mornings that warmed into comfortable, short-lived afternoons.

Lost in thought, she pushed aside the comforter and padded barefoot across the old wooden floor. Zipp turned his head briefly to acknowledge her presence beside him at the window, then returned to stare fixedly out into the shadows.

"What's the matter, Zipp? Do you envy him? Want to go outside and do a little night hunting? I knew sooner or later you'd miss the old days. He reminds you of them, doesn't he?" Rani smiled wistfully at her cat. "I'm not surprised. I thought of you the minute I saw him standing on my doorstep in the pouring rain, demanding shelter and a meal. And like a fool I gave him both, just as I gave them to you. But at least you've got enough sense to come in out of the cold. Apparently Flint doesn't." She straightened away from the window and reached for her coat and a pair of shoes. "Come on, we'd better go and bring him inside before he catches a chill."

She flung the trench coat over her long-sleeved, ankle-length nightgown, slipped into her leather loafers and started down the hall. Zipp bounced off the windowsill to trot at her heels. When Rani reached the kitchen and opened the back door, the cat dashed past her into the darkness, alert to the kind of excitement only night can bring a cat. Rani followed more slowly, wondering what sort of excitement the shadows brought Flint Cottrell. Memories of past hunting expeditions? She knew without giving the matter much thought that if Flint had ever gone hunting it wouldn't have been for the usual game. He wasn't one to take pleasure in killing animals. She remembered the scar on his shoulder: it was a good bet a human opponent had been the cause.

She found him around the corner of the house. He was apparently studying the broken brick walk in the pale moonlight, the collar of his sheepskin jacket pulled close around his neck. His head was bare as usual as he bent to examine the path, and his hands were thrust deep into the pockets of his jacket. Rani knew he was aware of her presence as she slowly approached, but he didn't look up.

"It's cold out here. You'd better get back inside," Flint said without looking at her.

Rani's chin lifted as she huddled into the trench coat. "Interestingly enough, that's just what I was about to say to you. What in the world are you doing running around outside at midnight, Flint?"

"Thinking."

"Oh, that explains it," she assured him dryly. "Do you always do your best thinking when you're freezing?"

"I wasn't doing any decent thinking at all indoors. I decided to try a walk in the garden." His voice was edged with annoyance as he finally turned his head to look at her. "Any objections?"

"Yes, plenty of them. You're disturbing my cat, for one thing."

Flint scowled. "Zipp? What the hell's wrong with him?"

Rani half smiled. "I'm afraid seeing you abroad in the moonlight has brought back memories of his own free-wheeling past. When he saw you out here he couldn't wait to get outside himself. But I don't believe he's using the opportunity to think. He's probably hunting. Lord knows what he'll bring into the house tomorrow morning."

Flint watched her for a long moment. "If he does bring something home, he'll expect you to tell him what a terrific hunter he is."

"No doubt."

"You will, won't you, Rani?" Flint suddenly sounded quite certain. "You'll scold him at first and then you'll relent and tell him how magnificent he is."

"I don't see what all this has to do with your being out here at midnight. What were you trying to think about?" Rani took a couple of steps closer to him, attempting to read his eyes in the shadowed light. The gaze that was so unusually green in the daytime, however, was mysteriously lacking in color tonight. She couldn't begin to guess at his thoughts.

"I was trying to work on the article."

"I see. It's not going well?"

"It's not going at all," Flint growled. "I was sitting there surrounded by a ton of notes and I couldn't write page one. I've been thinking about this article for a long time. I know the facts cold. But it isn't going nearly as smoothly as it should. Not like the others I've written. Tonight I couldn't even figure out how to write the first sentence."

Rani heard the frustration in his voice and impulsively reached out to touch his jacket sleeve. "Are you a night person?"

Flint eyed her warily, and she continued, "Is that when your thinking is clear? Is that when your biological time clock is at its peak?"

Flint shrugged. "Lady, I don't know what you're talking about. All I know is that I couldn't even make a start on that damn article tonight."

"And now you're tense." Rani tugged lightly at his sleeve. "Come inside, Flint. I'll make us some hot cocoa and then we can discuss your problem."

She wasn't surprised when he followed without protest. Any offer of food seemed to hold a definite allure for Flint. Silently he allowed her to lead him into the kitchen where he took off his jacket. Then, his gaze following Rani's every movement as she set about making hot cocoa, he sprawled on a chair with an unconscious, arrogant grace.

Leaving her trench coat on as a makeshift robe, Rani switched on the stove and measured milk into a pan. "Now, about this biological time clock, Flint."

"What about it?"

"I was under the impression you're an early riser."

"I am. So what?"

"Well, so am I."

"Something in common," he murmured a little too blandly.

Rani disregarded his tone of voice. "Exactly. Now, we early risers generally have something else in common. We usually do our best work, regardless of what it is, in the morning. What sort of work were you doing bright and early this morning?"

"You know damn well what I was doing. I was raking leaves, hauling rocks and pushing a wheelbarrow."

Rani turned to glance at him, her smile triumphant. "Precisely my point. You put most of your energy into hard physical labor today, using up your best hours on that kind of thing instead of on your article. Then you wonder why you can't seem to get it together at midnight to do your writing." She stirred briskly. "Want some advice?"

"I'm listening."

"Get up early and do your writing in the morning. Save the gardening and repair work for after lunch. You've got several weeks to get the grounds in shape and fix the odds and ends that need repairing. Use your evenings to relax and get some sleep." She poured the cocoa into mugs and brought them to the table.

"Is this valid scientific fact or pop psychology?"

"Trust me. It works." Rani sipped at the hot drink. "Tomorrow morning get out of bed bright and early, have your breakfast, pour yourself a cup of coffee and then go to work on your article. At lunchtime you can quit and start the outside work."

Flint looked at her over the rim of his mug. "You know, you're sweet when you're giving orders."

"Nobody said you had to follow them," she retorted.

"Ah, but I do. For now at any rate. You're wearing the ring, remember? Maybe I'm the man fated to be drawn under your spell."

"The ring," she announced grandly, "is phony, remember? Besides, you don't believe in legends. You're a professional debunker of tall tales."

"Who knows?" There was amusement in his face, even though the hard line of his mouth hadn't crooked into a smile. "The fact remains I seem to find myself doing what I'm told these days."

"Thank you. I'll treasure that compliment."

They sipped the cocoa in a surprisingly companionable silence for a while, and then Rani remembered the question she had been meaning to ask. "How did you come to know about Uncle Ambrose and this ring, Flint?"

Flint shifted slightly in his chair. Rani wasn't sure, but she thought some of the relaxation engendered by the cocoa had abruptly faded. It seemed to her there was a certain tension in him now as he studied his mug.

"Ambrose and I ran into each other a year and a half ago when the ring came into his possession."

"Uncle Ambrose bought the ring?" Rani raised an eyebrow in astonishment. "Or was it stolen by one of his confederates?"

Flint shook his head once, a short, brusque gesture that told her nothing. "What does it matter now? He and I never discussed exactly how he had acquired the thing, but there was no doubt it was a favorite object of his. At any rate, he'd come across an article I once did for a gem trade magazine. Just a short piece giving a history of the ring, not a major article like the one I'm doing now. He wanted to know more about it so he tracked me down through the publisher. As it happened, I'd just submitted another piece to that same publisher and he knew where he could get in touch with me. He gave me Ambrose's address in New York and I contacted him. I was just as interested in finding out who now owned the ring as he was in learning more about its history. Ambrose and I got along fine. He was a real character. I liked him, Rani."

Rani smiled. "Most people did, I gather. It was one of the reasons he was so successful. A natural con man probably. I only met Ambrose a few times. I never really got to know him. He never married. My father's side of the family was always very scattered and out of touch. I was quite surprised when I discovered he'd left all that wonderful fake jewelry to me. It's really beautiful stuff. Probably his finest work."

"What else was there besides the ring?"

"A great necklace that looks as if it came out of an Egyptian pyramid, a couple of pairs of earrings set with such beautifully cut paste that most people would mistake them for diamonds. A couple of other rings besides this one and a brooch.''

"And you had them all appraised?''

Rani nodded. "My uncle had a business acquaintance in San Francisco. His name's Charles Dewhurst and he's a gemologist. Dewhurst had occasionally referred customers who wanted a high-quality reproduction to my uncle. He knew nothing about the shady side of Ambrose's business, of course. Few people did. He was as shocked as everyone else to learn about it after my uncle was killed. But, like you, he'd been fond of Uncle Ambrose and he greatly respected his talent. Mr. Dewhurst contacted my father after he learned of my uncle's death and offered his condolences. Said that whatever else Ambrose had been, he was one of the finest craftsman in the world. When I received the jewelry, I decided to have someone who was familiar with my uncle's work take a look at the stuff.''

"And Dewhurst confirmed it was junk?''

"Very beautiful junk,'' Rani corrected with a smile. "But, nevertheless, fake. Apparently Uncle Ambrose had kept his finest pieces for himself.''

"I wonder what he did with the real stone that was originally in that ring,'' Flint mused.

"Probably recut and sold it for a tidy fortune,'' Rani grinned. "Or perhaps it now belongs to a successful jewel thief.''

Flint downed the last of his cocoa and sat cradling the mug between his large hands. "I think the setting might, at least, be original,'' he said slowly.

"Why do you say that?''

"Because the damn thing seems to be working on me.'' He lifted his gaze to her suddenly wary face. "Perhaps there's a little magic left in the ring, even though the stone itself has been replaced. What do you think, Rani?''

"I think," she said very carefully, "that's a strange thing for a man who doesn't believe in legends to say. I also think that it's time for both of us to get some sleep. It's almost one o'clock, Flint."

"I know." He got to his feet when she did, but he made no move to go to the door.

"Flint." She should exercise whatever small power she did possess to order him out of her kitchen. This business of feeding strays at midnight was very dangerous. The tension that was suddenly filling the room was rapidly replacing the cozy warmth. She felt it thrumming along her nerves, urging her to take a step or two forward. Steps that would bring her very close to Flint. He was a vibrant, masculine presence in her kitchen, filling the room with his particular brand of strength.

"I'm the one under the spell, Rani," he whispered huskily. "You're in control, remember? I can't take any more than you want to give."

She clutched the lapels of the trench coat. "What do you want from me, Flint?"

"A little warmth. A little gentleness. I've been restless a long time. I want some peace and comfort." He moved toward her, a soft, gliding step that closed the distance between them. "I need it. I've never needed anything this badly."

Rani felt his arms going around her, drawing her against him until her palms flattened on his shoulders. She couldn't seem to tear her own eyes from the banked, emerald fires in his. She should stay in control, she reminded herself. It was her nature to avoid risks. Now here she was suddenly on the verge of being drawn into a green vortex of excitement. She mustn't let that happen. She must stay on the edge of the storm and not let herself be whirled into its heart.

But a part of her was longing to sample a bit of the green fire. Her face lifted as Flint brought his mouth down on hers. The arms wrapped around her were heavy and strong and made her feel unexpectedly secure. Her palms moved up over his shoulders and around his neck.

The heat and the need in Flint beat at Rani in waves. She could feel it in every inch of his hard body. As his mouth moved hungrily against hers, she realized just how much self-control he was calling upon, and the knowledge that he was doing so reassured her somehow. When Flint's tongue probed at the edge of her lips, seeking entrance, she opened her mouth to him.

He groaned as the kiss became hot, damp and intimate. Rani felt Flint's hands kneading the small of her back, his fingers sliding down to find the shape of her buttocks. She shivered beneath the onslaught of powerful, sensual sensations that were startlingly new to her, even though she was far from being a naive teenager. He felt the tremor that rippled through her and pulled her deeper into the heat of his thighs.

When Rani murmured his name far back in her throat, Flint shifted her so that she was cradled in one of his arms. He didn't break the fierce kiss as he used his free hand to find the belt of the trench coat. Rani felt the edges of the coat part, and before she could decide how to deal with the new level of initimacy, Flint's hand was on her breast.

"Rani, I want you. I'm beginning to think I've always wanted you."

She heard the rough urgency in his words and couldn't tell if he were pleading or stating some irrefutable fact of life. Either way it wreaked havoc with her senses. Her fingertips curled in the fine hair at the base of his neck, scoring him very gently with her nails. She could feel the strength in his shoulders, and it tantalized her. When his thumb moved across one of her nipples, coaxing it forth beneath the fabric of her nightgown, she shuddered and pressed closer.

"That's right, honey. This is the way it has to be." Flint freed her lips, continuing to talk to her in low, dark tones as he brushed his mouth across her cheek and down the line of her throat. The words were timeless, heavy with passion, thick with masculine hunger. Rani felt them sink into her, adding fuel to the fires he was building with every touch.

When the front of the nightgown opened, Rani barely felt it. But when Flint's fingers traced the shape of her breast, she nestled her head against his shoulder. She could feel the hardening lines of his body as he pulled her closer.

"Rani, look at me. Let me see your eyes," Flint ordered softly.

She lifted her head, feeling dazed and unfocused. He studied her face for a long moment and then nodded as if satisfied. He fit his hands to her throat and held her still for another kiss. Then he brought her slowly, deliberately against him so that the peaking tips of her bare breasts were pushed against his wool sweater. The sensation was exquisitely teasing. Rani sucked in her breath.

"This is only the beginning, sweetheart. Only the beginning." Flint ran his palms down her arms. His expression was full of sensual promise.

"Flint?" From out of nowhere, Rani remembered her own words about the dangers of feeding stray cats. There was danger here, in her kitchen now. As if her thoughts had summoned up the interruption, a whining meow sounded outside the kitchen door. Rani stilled and then turned her head. It was a shock to realize she was standing half-naked in Flint's arms.

"It's all right, Rani." Flint touched her hair, twining his fingers through the spice-colored thickness of it. "I'm going to take you to bed and everything will be all right."

The demanding meow sounded again outside the door. Rani stepped backward, seeking escape. Somewhat to her surprise, Flint didn't try to stop her. Hastily she retied the belt of the trench coat, aware of the flush of heat in her face.

"Rani?"

"It's Zipp. He wants to come back inside."

"Yes." Flint's eyes never moved from her strained face. "He'll always want to come back inside. Just as I will."

She shook her head, trying to clear it. "I dont quite know what to say. This probably shouldn't have happened. I . . . I shouldn't have allowed it to happen."

"I don't think either of us had any choice."

That struck a chord. "I don't believe in fate and I doubt that you do, either. You're the one who writes articles illustrating the falseness of old legends, remember?"

"Yes, ma'am."

"Oh, for heaven's sake. You'd better get back to your own cottage. It's very late and you're going to need sleep if you're to try the new writing schedule tomorrow." She glared at him, brow drawn together in a ferocious line.

"I hear you, lady."

"I want you up bright and early."

"Yes, ma'am."

"If you say that one more time, I won't be responsible for my actions!"

"Yes, ma—I mean, good night, Rani. I'll let the cat in on my way out." He walked toward the door, his step soundless. When he opened the door, Zipp flicked his tail upward and walked haughtily into the room. His jaws were empty. Flint looked down at the cat. "No luck, Zipp? Well, don't feel bad. I didn't have much myself."

Before Rani could say anything suitably scathing, the door closed behind Flint.

The house felt empty the next morning. Rani opened her eyes and listened intently for the sound of clanging pots and pans. She heard nothing, which was exactly what she should be hearing, she reminded herself bracingly as she headed for the shower. She certainly didn't intend to spend the rest of her vacation fixing breakfast for Flint Cottrell. She ought to be glad he'd gotten the message.

The comfortable, stylishly baggy cotton trousers that nipped in at the waist and ankles were a neutral shade of off-white. They were one of the few neutrally shaded garments in Rani's closet. She offset the effect with a brilliant camp shirt patterned in orange-and-green jungle flowers. The look was supposed to be one of relaxed sophistication. Rani peered at herself in the mirror and couldn't decide if she'd pulled off the desired style or not. She'd achieved her usual loud impact, however. She clipped her hair into a loose coil on top of her head and headed down the hall to prepare herself a peaceful breakfast.

Zipp was already in the kitchen ahead of her, sunning himself on the windowsill. He flipped an inquiring ear in her direction as she opened the refrigerator door.

"Did you have a good time running around in the middle of the night?" Rani asked as she fixed a bowl of cereal for herself. The cat didn't bother to reply. "I noticed you didn't stay out very long last night. What happened? Decide a warm bed was a better option than a cold night of hunting? Better watch it, cat. You might be getting soft and civilized."

Zipp appeared neither soft nor civilized as he stretched out his battered frame in the sunlight, but he did look decidedly content. Rani thought about that for a moment, wondering how old the cat was. He had been full grown when she'd adopted him, so she had no certain knowledge of his age. He'd just appeared out of nowhere one rainy night at her home in Santa Rosa. But he still had the strength and agility of an animal in the prime of its life, so she didn't think he was old.

"A mature cat who knew a good thing when he saw it, huh, Zipp? Is that what you were when you landed on my doorstep and demanded a meal?"

Zipp began the deep rumbling that, for him, passed for a purr. Then he rolled off the windowsill, landed on all four feet on the counter and dived for the floor. He ambled across the room and stood waiting impatiently to have the kitchen door opened for him. With a sigh, Rani obediently got to her feet and performed the service.

She watched him stalk out into the chilly sunlight. A moment later it became obvious where he was heading: straight for Flint's cottage. Rani leaned in the doorway, sipping her coffee and watching as the animal lazily made his way through the garden. A few moments later he reached the front step of the cottage. Rani didn't hear the demanding meow, but it wasn't long before Flint opened the door.

He looked across the garden as he stood waiting for the cat to enter. When he saw Rani, Flint nodded a solemn good morning and then shut the door. Cat and man disappeared.

So Flint was up and apparently working. Rani considered that, aware of a pleased sense of satisfaction. She could only hope he was accomplishing something. Smiling a little to herself, she shut her own door and started in on the few chores required in her vacation home.

An hour later there was still no sign of Flint. He wasn't in the garden, and she hadn't heard the Jeep leave. She had to assume he was still working. Curiosity began to get the better of Rani's sense of discretion. She put down the British-style mystery she had been reading and wandered out into the rapidly warming day. It came as no great surprise to find herself standing outside Flint's door a short time later. Rani stood still, listening for the clack of a typewriter. She heard nothing, and when Flint opened the door without any warning, she jumped a good half foot.

"Sorry, didn't mean to startle you," he apologized idly, studying her with grave interest. "What are you doing out here? Listening at keyholes?"

"I just came to ransom my cat."

"You'll have to wake him up, first. He's sleeping on top of my desk." Flint stood back, silently inviting her into the small cottage.

A little warily Rani stepped over the threshold. "Your desk?"

"I turned the kitchen table into one." He closed the door and nodded toward the room's single table. A small portable electric typewriter stood in the center. It was surrounded by notebooks, paper and several weighty texts.

Rani cast a quick eye over the lot, ignoring Zipp who was, indeed, sound asleep between a dictionary and a thick, leather-bound tome. "Any luck? Writing, I mean?"

Flint smiled slightly, his eyes on her curious face. "Foolhardy as it probably is, I have to admit you were right. When I sat down this morning, things came much easier. My thinking was far more organized."

Rani grinned, pleased with herself. "Well, there you are then. You're on your way to fame and fortune. I'd better not keep you from your work."

He shook his head, moving over to the stove to turn the heat on under a dented steel kettle. "I was just about to take a break. Want some coffee?"

Rani hesitated and then nodded. "All right." She wandered over to the littered table. "Where will you submit the article when you're done with it?"

He shrugged. "Probably *Legends and Fantasy*. They bought the last couple of things I did. If they don't take it, I might try *Treasure Lore*."

Rani nodded. "We get both of them at the branch library where I work. They're quite popular. Kids like them. So do adults who daydream about going treasure hunting."

"My audience awaits," he said dryly. "All I have to do is get it written. I'm beginning to think the problem with this article is that I might be becoming, uh, emotionally involved with my work."

"Since you claim you don't believe in legends, you'd better be careful about becoming too involved," Rani tried to say lightly.

Flint gave her an enigmatic look. "The catch is that if there's any truth to the legend I don't have any choice."

Rani stared unseeingly down at the sheaf of papers on the table, her senses strangely ruffled into almost painful alertness by the underlying edge in his words. "Flint, I'm not looking for a one-night or even a one-month stand."

"You're a woman who doesn't take chances."

"And you're a man who's accustomed to taking them?" she whispered.

"For as long as I can remember," he agreed.

The shrill whistle of the old kettle demanded his attention. Flint reached for two mugs and spooned instant coffee into them. There was a tense silence in the small cottage as he prepared the brew. Then he picked up the mugs and handed one to Rani.

"Going to spend your whole life looking for a sure thing?" he asked, green eyes steady.

She resented the implied criticism. "Perhaps," Rani said coolly. "What about you? Going to spend your whole life leaping from one job, one adventure, to another?"

"People change, Rani."

"When?"

"When they find what they're looking for, I guess."

"I'd have to be awfully sure," she said cautiously.

"Before you'd take a real chance on a man?"

"Yes."

"When you're dealing with human beings, there aren't any certainties."

"That's probably especially true when dealing with a man whose track record doesn't exactly provide evidence of stability," she retorted, feeling trapped.

"What about that artist you're seeing here in Reed Lake? You think he's the stable type?"

"No," she admitted. "But with him it doesn't matter."

Flint smiled gently. "With me it does?"

Rani's mouth went dry as she realized the truth of her own words. "Yes," she said bluntly. "It does."

"I can't give you any guarantees."

"I know."

"I realize my track record isn't exactly reassuring."

"You're right."

"But I'm not a boy. I've been looking for something for a long time. Something it takes a man to recognize."

"You think you've found it?"

"I think so. But the lady is going to have to take a chance, too, before either of us can be certain."

Rani moved uneasily beneath the steady regard of his green gaze. "Don't you think this is an odd discussion to be having after only knowing each other such a short period of time?"

He looked at her intently. "What's time got to do with it?"

Rani's mouth tightened with feminine resentment. "You expect me to simply hop into bed with you, don't you? Do you have any conception of just how much you're asking?''

"Sure. I'm asking you to take a chance on a man who doesn't fit your image of male perfection. But no man ever will fit it, Rani, so why should I give up and humbly depart? I want what you've got to offer and I don't think you're ever going to find someone who will appreciate it more than I will." He paused, considering his own words and then added with brutal honesty. "Even if I did think you stood a chance of finding a man who would appreciate it more, I'm not inclined to leave the field open for him. Us stray alley cats have developed a habit of looking out for ourselves first."

"How can you possibly know what you want or what I'm prepared to offer? And why in the hell would I want an alley cat of a man in the first place?" Rani blazed. "You're absolutely right, you don't fit my image of the ideal mate. No fixed address, no fixed job and no fixed future." She was working herself into a fine, righteous temper, but Flint seemed oblivious.

"I don't care about the fixed address or the fixed job. I've relied on my wits long enough to know I can take care of myself. But I am in the market for a permanent woman. I'm ready for a home, Rani. A fixed future."

"But that's ridiculous!"

"Why? I told you, I'm a man, not a boy. I can recognize what I want when I find it."

"You hardly know me," she wailed indignantly.

"Before either of us can be sure, you're going to have to take a chance on me."

Rani caught her breath at the masculine command buried in the words. She was almost physically aware of his willpower reaching out to grapple with hers, and the sensation was frightening. Frantically she summoned up her self-control.

"I think," she managed with a cool poise she was far from feeling, "that you'd better get back to work. I wouldn't want to get in the way of your excellent start."

"Want to hear a few of the tales surrounding that ring you're wearing?"

"No, I do not." Rani moved imperiously to the door, setting her mug down on the tiny drainboard.

"Some other time? Say, over dinner?"

Rani paused at the door, exceedingly grateful for her previous engagement. Ruthlessly she willed herself to ignore the hopefulness in his voice. "I'm going out to dinner tonight."

"That damn artist."

"Yes." The single word was almost a hiss.

"What time will you be back?"

Her eyes widened. "I haven't the faintest idea. I might not be back until morning!"

He grinned at that, a fleeting, amused, thoroughly wicked expression that contained far too much masculine arrogance and more than a hint of real danger. "You'll be back at a decent hour."

"Or what?" she challenged recklessly.

"Or I'll come looking for you."

"Get back to your typewriter, Flint." She slammed the door but not before she heard his laconic last words.

"Yes, ma'am."

Four

___

Dinner had been an enjoyable occasion, but as Mike Slater parked his nondescript little Ford compact in Rani's driveway, matters started to disintegrate. Rani stared at the light shining through the curtains of her living room windows and frowned.

"I don't recall turning on the lights before I left this evening," she remarked as Mike opened the car door for her.

"Maybe you just forgot to switch them off when I picked you up tonight." Mike glanced toward the house.

"No, I would have remembered." Rani sighed as she dug her key out of her shoulder bag. "My neighbor was probably raiding my refrigerator."

Mike's brow lifted inquiringly. "I didn't know you had a neighbor."

"He's a handyman or gardener or something. The Andersons hired him to put things in shape around here. He's staying in the back cottage."

"You didn't mention him."

Rani shrugged as she pushed open the front door. "He just arrived a couple days ago. I guess I forgot to tell you about him." There was a sharp hiss of annoyance from Zipp, who took one look at the stranger standing next to Rani and promptly disappeared.

Flint's voice called out from the kitchen. "Hey, you two are back early. Want some coffee? I just made a pot." He sauntered to the kitchen doorway and stood leaning against the frame, a suspiciously bland smile on his hard face as he looked at Mike. He was wearing a dark long-sleeved shirt with the sleeves rolled up casually on his forearms. His jeans were faded and worn, and he had on a pair of low, scuffed boots. Standing there with a coffeepot in one hand, he looked very much at home, intimidatingly so. He seemed aware of it. "You must be the artist."

Mike blinked but rose to the occasion. He kept his voice just as politely dry as Flint's had been. "You must be the handyman or gardener or something."

Flint nodded agreeably. "That's me. Very handy. Here I am standing here with hot coffee just as you walk in the door. Where else are you going to get that kind of service?"

Rani stepped forward aggressively and took the pot from his hand. "This sort of thing isn't on your list of job duties and you know it," she muttered furiously, sweeping past him into the kitchen. "You've got your own kitchen. Kindly stay out of mine."

"Not my fault you walked in just as I was making the coffee."

"Really?" She smiled dangerously as she hauled cups out of the cupboard. "How long have you been here?"

Flint shrugged, ignoring Mike. "I came over to find something to read earlier and decided to make the coffee."

"Uh-huh. In other words you've been here all evening."
Rani swung around, two coffee cups in her hands. "Excuse
me, Flint, you're in the way." She moved forward, silently
daring him not to move out of the doorway. When he
stepped aside, she hid her relief. "Here you are, Mike. Come
on into the living room and sit down. Flint was just leaving."

"Actually," said Flint, "I wouldn't mind joining you. It's
been a long, quiet evening. I'm Flint Cottrell, by the way."
He nodded at the other man.

"Mike Slater." Mike glanced at him and then smiled
quizzically at Rani. "Maybe I'd better be on my way." He
left it a question.

"Don't rush off on my account." Flint sprawled in a
chair, a mug of coffee in his hand. Zipp immediately appeared from wherever he had been sulking and hopped into
Flint's lap. After a few glares in Mike's direction, the cat finally settled down to a machine-gun purr. "You two have a
nice evening?" Flint said conversationally.

"It's been lovely up until now." Rani urged her guest to
a chair. Mike sat down somewhat reluctantly and accepted
the cup and saucer she handed him.

"We went to the resort at the far end of the lake," Mike
said politely. "Good steaks."

Rani's smile was determined. "Good band, too."

"The place was probably full of deer hunters," Flint observed, oblivious to the chill in her voice.

"Not really," Rani said. Mostly resort guests. The only
signs of the hunters were the rifle shots we heard between
here and the resort."

Mike nodded, frowning. "It was just at dusk. Some
hunter must have been making one last try for a deer before
nightfall. He was too near the road if you ask me. We could
hear the shots quite clearly."

"Crazy hunters. No common sense," Rani complained. "They have no business shooting that close to civilization."

"Every hunting season someone gets hurt," Mike said. "Usually another hunter. It's a dangerous sport."

Rani grimaced. "Frankly, my sympathy is with the deer."

Flint looked at Mike. "You come up here to Reed Lake regularly?"

"I usually head for the mountains at this time of the year," Mike acknowledged politely. "Spent last winter in Tahoe and the winter before that in Lake County. I like mountains in winter."

Rani smiled, doing her best to shut Flint out of the conversation. "Are mountains in winter good for the creative juices?"

"I do some of my best work during winter."

Flint smiled blandly again. "Being an artist must be a lot like being a handyman. Not too stable a profession."

"Oh, I work on a regular basis," Mike assured him. "I show relatively often and have a fairly steady following. I haven't been a starving artist for a very long time."

"Where do you show?" Flint asked.

"Down in the Bay area and Carmel mostly. Why? Are you interested in art?"

"In a way. I'm in the process of changing careers, you see," Flint told him.

"I see." Mike tried to look politely interested.

Rani decided it was time to step in and regain control of the situation. "Well, I don't. There's not much connection between painting and career hunting."

"Sure there is," Flint said, looking offended. "They're both creative efforts, aren't they?"

"Perhaps you should be making a bit more of a creative effort," she suggested coolly as she glanced pointedly at her watch. "In fact, maybe it's time you went back to work."

Flint shook his head. "Not tonight. I've taken your advice and given up trying to write at night." His green eyes glittered between his narrowed lashes as he looked at Mike. "Rani prefers me to work during the day and keep my evenings free."

Patience exhausted, Rani set down her cup and saucer with a clatter and got to her feet. "Good night, Flint."

He looked up at her. "I haven't finished my coffee."

"Take it with you."

"What's the rush, honey? It's not that late."

Before Rani could respond, Mike was getting to his feet, mild embarrassment on his lean face. "Uh, maybe I'd better be on my way, too. It is getting kind of late. Thanks for a great evening, Rani. I'll probably see you at the post office in town tomorrow."

"There's no need to leave," Rani said grimly. "Flint was just on his way out."

Flint stretched hugely, putting down his mug. "You're right, Slater. It is late."

"Yes, well, see you tomorrow, Rani." Mike was already at the door.

Rani shot a glare at Flint and hurried forward. "I'll walk outside with you." She let the door close behind herself and Mike and wound up standing on the porch, smiling apologetically at her date for the evening. "I'm sorry about that. He's a very strange man. Just sort of moves in and makes himself at home."

"Where did he come from?" Mike looked down at her, bracing himself with one hand against the porch railing.

"Beats me. Here, there and everywhere from the sound of things. I asked him about his previous jobs and he implied he's had a lot of them. Very unstable."

"I hope that applies to his job history and not his psychological profile."

Rani's eyes widened. She rubbed her forearms with her palms. "Surely you don't think he's dangerous?"

Mike looked immediately chagrined. "No, of course not. I don't know anything about the man, do I? It's just that you made him sound weird and he does seem to have assumed he's got a right to wander in and out of your house without permission. That's hardly the behavior of the average handyman."

"I wouldn't know. I haven't met too many handymen." Rani tried a nervous smile. "Or gardeners either, for that matter. Actually, he's also a part-time writer of some sort. Does articles for magazines, or so he says."

"What kind of articles does he write?"

"Articles about legends."

"Legends?"

"Umm." Rani held up her hand so that the porch light gleamed dully off the green stone in her ring. "Legends concerning things like this ring, which he thinks might be very old."

Mike took a closer look at the ring. "He's interested in this rock?"

"He says it's one of the reasons he's here. Oh, it's a long story. The bottom line is that this ring once belonged to my Uncle Ambrose who died earlier this year. Flint knows the history of the ring, and when he decided to write his article he wanted to see what happened to it. He found out it had been left to me." She broke off at the odd expression on Mike's face.

"Rani, are you telling me the man got a job here just to be near the ring?"

She swallowed uneasily. "Put like that, it does sound rather strange, doesn't it? But I think it's the truth. There's nothing really menacing about his actions. He's just a . . . a different sort of man."

"Is the ring valuable?" Mike asked sharply.

"Oh, no," she hastened to assure him. "At least not from a jeweler's point of view. The stone is paste. I had it appraised. Besides, have you ever seen a real emerald this size?"

Mike grinned. "Are you kidding? I don't shop at the kind of stores that sell emeralds that size."

"Neither do I." She waved her hand airily. "It's junk. Pretty yes, but junk nevertheless. The only value is in the legend, and that's why Flint is interested in it."

"How valuable is the legend to him?" Mike asked flatly.

"He says the ring can only be worn by a woman. He's not likely to steal it."

Mike ran a hand through his hair and shook his head. "I don't know, Rani. It's a strange setup."

"I know. But I honestly don't think it's a dangerous one."

Mike hesitated. "As long as you're sure."

"I'm sure."

Mike glanced away. "Am I, uh, stepping into his territory?"

"His territory?"

"Yeah. I don't want to get involved in a touchy situation. If you and he are, uh . . ."

"We most definitely are *not*." Rani's eyes narrowed. "And you are not stepping on his turf. I don't conduct my social life on that primitive a level. I date whom I wish and I am not *involved* with anyone. Clear?"

Mike nodded quickly. "Very clear. Sorry about that. I just wanted to know where you stood."

Rani forgave him immediately. He appeared thoroughly abashed. "Don't worry about it. I know how it must have looked, the way Flint was hanging around my kitchen with the coffeepot. The problem is that the cottage he's got is in very poor condition. It hasn't been used in years, and he probably hasn't even got a coffeepot." That wasn't strictly true. He had a kettle in which he could boil hot water for instant coffee, but Rani thought she wouldn't go into too much detail.

"Well, in that case, do I dare risk asking for another date?"

She laughed up at him. "You bet. I had a wonderful time tonight, Mike. Thanks very much." She started to stand on tiptoe so that he could give her a polite good-night kiss, but at that moment the door opened behind her. She closed her eyes in disgust and sighed.

"Isn't it getting a little chilly out here?" Flint asked cheerily.

Mike nodded. "A little. I'll be on my way." He trotted down the steps and got into the Ford.

Rani stood watching until the small Ford had disappeared from the drive. Then she turned to confront Flint who was standing in the doorway with Zipp at his feet. Slowly she gathered herself, struggling to keep her temper under control. She would not lose it, she vowed. She would be cold and disdainful and not give into the temptation to yell at him like a fishwife. The vow lasted all of five seconds.

"Of all the rude, insufferable, socially inept people I have ever met in my life, you take the honors, Flint Cottrell. You should be ashamed of yourself. You had no business being here when I got home with Mike. And no business forcing yourself on us while we had our coffee. Who do you think you are? Didn't you learn manners anywhere along the line, or have you spent so much time hopping around the globe that you neglected to learn the basics? No wonder you don't stay long in any one place. You're probably asked to leave when you start becoming impossible.'' She was starting to yell. She knew she was. Savagely she bit off the last words and stormed past Flint into the living room.

Flint slowly closed the door and turned to face her. He didn't say anything. He seemed to be waiting. That infuriated Rani even more. She flung herself down on the old, padded sofa and scowled. ''I suppose you've got an explanation for your behaviour?''

''I was waiting for you.''

She gritted her teeth. ''Why?''

''You know why, Rani.'' He spoke softly, moving silently across the room to collect the used coffee cups.

''No, I don't know why. I'm thirty years old. I've been handling my social life all by myself for a long time. I don't appreciate some heavy-handed big brother type waiting around for me when I come in the door.''

''I'm not the big brother type so you can stop worrying.''

''That's the way you were acting tonight.''

He shook his head, walking into the kitchen. ''No.''

She jumped to her feet and went after him. Halting in the kitchen doorway, she eyed him with suppressed violence as he put the dishes in the sink. ''Then how would you describe your own behaviour?''

He kept his attention on the cups he was putting into the sink, but his expression grew thoughtful. ''Possessive might be a good description. Protective. Concerned.''

Rani held her breath as he said the words. She sensed the tension in him, knew it communicated itself to her. "You have no right, Flint."

He turned his head to look at her, his green eyes unfathomable. "I also have no choice."

"What's that supposed to mean?"

"I can't let another man make love to you, Rani. Not now. I've been searching for you for too long. It would drive me crazy to know someone else was touching you now that I've found you."

She stared at him. "I think you already are a little crazy."

He didn't move. "You don't believe that."

"Mike suggested it might be a possibility," she said recklessly. "I told him about the ring and why you were working here this winter. You've got to admit, it does sound strange, Flint. And your behavior doesn't exactly make it seem less strange."

He ignored that. "What did he say about the ring?"

"He asked if it was valuable. I think he was worried you might try to steal it."

"You gave him your opinion that it was strictly paste?"

This wasn't the direction she had intended to take the conversation, Rani thought wildly. "It's not just my opinion! I had the thing appraised. I keep telling you that."

"Did you tell Slater that?"

"Yes, damn it! Will you forget about the stupid ring? It's not an issue here."

"What is the issue?" he asked interestedly.

"Your rude and objectionable behavior."

"Oh, that."

"Yes, that." Rani threw up her hands in surrender. "I've about had if for tonight, Flint. It's obvious you have no intention of listening to what I say or in apologizing. Kindly go back to your cottage and leave me in peace."

He came toward her, his big hands lifting to settle heavily on her shoulders. Flint smiled with a touch of genuine sympathy. "Poor Rani. You're used to being in command of your life, aren't you?"

"Nothing has changed. I am in command of my life. I intend to remain so. Get out of here, Flint. In case you haven't noticed, I am angry and disgusted. I would like some peace and quiet. Maybe I'm the one who's a little crazy. I must be for tolerating your behavior."

"Rani—"

"I mean it, Flint. I want you to leave."

He hesitated. Rani could feel the weight and strength in his hands. Such big hands. They were hard and callused from a lifetime of rough work. She didn't want to think about what those hands might feel like on her body. She would not allow herself to think about such things. She really would drive herself crazy. Rani could feel Flint's willpower pushing against her own. He wanted her to back down, wanted her to retreat and relax. She knew without having to hear the words that he wanted to stay the night. He seemed to think he had a right. It took far more of her own willpower than it should have to resist the possessive demands that flamed in his green gaze.

"Maybe not tonight, Rani, but sometime soon," Flint said quietly. "It has to be soon. I want you."

"What you want," she got out between clenched teeth, "has nothing to do with it."

"You'll want it, too. I swear it."

"That sounds like a typical male ego talking."

"How long are you going to fight me, Rani?"

"As long as necessary. Now go, Flint."

He wanted to kiss her. She waited tensely, not certain what would happen if he did. It would be so much easier if he didn't. Rani was more afraid of her own reactions than his actions. A kiss could be such a casual, meaningless thing. It would have been casual and meaningless with Mike, for example. She was sure of that. But it was altogether different with Flint. That made the prospect seem very dangerous.

But he didn't kiss her. He stared down at her for a moment longer and then, very lightly, he brushed his fingertips across her lower lip. Rani trembled as she felt the roughness of his finger on the delicate tissue of her lips.

"I'll go, Rani. You can still send me away. But someday it won't be this easy. You know that, don't you?"

Easy, she thought wretchedly as he walked out the door. It would never be easy. But it was certainly necessary.

Zipp meowed plaintively at her feet. Rani glanced down at him as the back door closed behind Flint. "Don't look at me like that, cat. I'm in charge around here. I decide who stays and who goes."

Zipp looked unconvinced.

Rani awoke the next morning with an uneasy feeling that refused to recede. Restlessly she showered, then dressed in a pair of comfortable jeans and a black sweater that had big starbursts of yellow on the front and back. When she opened the refrigerator door to get a carton of skim milk for her cereal, the sunlight glanced sharply off the green stone in her ring. The gleam caught her eye, and she paused to look at the piece of jewelry.

It couldn't be valuable. Charles Dewhurst was a professional with years of experience. He couldn't have made a mistake about the stone in the ring. She wiggled her finger and watched the play of light on the surface of the green gem. It looked like nicely cut green glass to her. It had to be glass.

But if it were real that fact would change everything.

Rani chewed on her lower lip as she considered the ramifications of that thought. If the stone was genuine she had a problem. For one thing, she would have to stop viewing Flint Cottrell as an annoying, intriguing, unsettling male to whom she was attracted. She would have to view him as dangerous, just as Mike had suggested the night before.

It couldn't be real. Dewhurst couldn't have made a mistake.

Lost in thought, Rani closed the refrigerator door and went into the living room to stare at the phone. A phone call might reassure her, and heaven knew she could use some reassurance right now.

She didn't have Dewhurst's number, but it was easy enough to get it from information. Rani sat nervously on the edge of the sofa as the phone rang in Dewhurst's elegant little shop near Union Square in San Francisco. She could visualize him behind the counter, surrounded by the delicate tools of his trade, his balding head with its gray fringe bent over a fine ruby or a diamond necklace. Rani had only met him on the occasion when she had taken Ambrose's collection of jewelry in to be evaluated, but she had liked the short, stout Dewhurst. He had been cordial and helpful, happy to share the knowledge of her uncle's idiosyncracies. When he came on the line, Rani smiled in relief.

"Mr. Dewhurst, this is Rani Garroway. Ambrose Garroway's niece?"

"Of course, of course, Miss Garroway. How are you? Good to hear from you again. Are you enjoying your uncle's fine creations?"

"Very much. I get a kick out of wearing them, especially the green ring. You remember the ring?"

"Naturally. An excellent example of your uncle's art. Do take care of the setting, though. It's rather old, I'm afraid, and fragile. One of these days you're going to have to have the stone reset."

"Actually I'm calling about the stone, Mr. Dewhurst."

"Has it come loose already? I was sure that with care it was good for a while yet."

Rani idly touched the green stone with her finger. "It feels solid enough in the setting. That's not why I called."

"Then how can I help you, Miss Garroway?"

She hesitated and then took the plunge. "Mr. Dewhurst, there's no possibility that there's been a...mistake, is there?"

"A mistake?"

"I mean in the identification of the stone. It really is paste, isn't it?"

"Definitely." Dewhurst sounded regretful but absolutely positive. "Your uncle did a fine job on it, Miss Garroway, but it's definitely not an emerald. Ambrose wouldn't have been interested in a real emerald. He was a unique craftsman. He saw his skill as a talent for imitation and, you will excuse the term, deception. He took pride in his ability to make the false appear genuine."

"I know, it's just that lately I've had some questions from some acquaintances."

"Questions about the ring?"

"Someone suggested it might be the real thing," Rani admitted lamely, wishing she'd never called. This was getting embarrassing.

"Impossible." Dewhurst chuckled. "Not unless you've switched it with another since I last saw it. Once you've seen real emeralds, worked with them and studied them, it isn't easy to be deceived, Miss Garroway. I know this sounds melodramatic—jewelers sometimes get that way—but the fact is, a good quality, genuine emerald is like a bit of frozen green fire. It's almost hypnotic. One looks deeply into the stone and finds oneself having to make an effort to look away. Good emeralds are almost unbelievable, Miss Garroway. They take away one's breath. Believe me, I couldn't have made a mistake.''

Rani heard the conviction in his voice and smiled wryly to herself. He was right; he did sound impassioned on the subject. She held the ring up to the light again as she listened to Dewhurst. Squinting, she tried to determine if there was any possibility of there being flames of green fire locked inside the stone. She could see nothing of the sort.

It definitely looked like a beautiful cut green glass to her. Rani heaved a small inner sigh of relief. Of course it was glass. As she had told Mike the previous evening, no one saw emeralds this size outside of a classy jewelry store or a rich collector's safe-deposit box. Glass. Pretty green glass. With, perhaps, a legend attached.

"Someone mentioned to me the possibility of the ring having once been the focal point of a legend, Mr. Dewhurst. He said it was once called the Clayborne ring and that it dates back to the seventeen hundreds. Any chance the setting itself is that old?''

"As I recall, it appeared to date from the late eighteen hundreds. Possibly turn of the century. Not terribly old as these things go, but interesting, perhaps. Ambrose undoubtedly came into possession of the setting when he, uh, arranged to copy the stone that had once been in it.''

"So there might once have been a genuine emerald in this ring?''

"Quite possibly. It would make sense that if Ambrose created a replica, he would have faithfully copied the original. I don't see him having created a paste version of an emerald, for example, if the stone in the ring had once been a ruby or a sapphire. He took pains to duplicate exactly.''

"I see. But all things considered, the setting isn't more than a hundred years old?"

"If that."

"And the stone is definitely fake."

Dewhurst sighed. "I'm afraid so."

"Don't sound so sorry," Rani laughed. "Actually, the reassurance comes as a great relief. I would hate to think I'd been blithely waving a huge emerald around as though it were junk jewelry."

"There is no danger of that, Miss Garroway."

"Thanks, Mr. Dewhurst. I appreciate your time."

"I'm happy to have been of service."

Rani hung up the phone, feeling vastly relieved. Zipp meowed lazily, wandering in from the kitchen to inquire about his own breakfast. He saw Rani sitting on the sofa and meowed again, putting some demand into it.

"You are a bossy sort of cat, Zipp. What did you ever do before you had me to fetch and carry for you?"

Zipp watched her as she got to her feet. He trotted quickly after Rani as she went back into the kitchen, satisifed that breakfast was back on schedule.

Rani spent the morning working on a jigsaw puzzle, finished the mystery novel she had started and then wrote notes to friends. It occurred to her that she might be getting a trifle bored on vacation. It was a strange feeling. Normally she was quite content with her own company. Perhaps she would see about renting a rowboat to take out on the lake. The idea of going out in a boat made her think of picnic lunches, and picnic lunches made her think of sharing the outing with someone.

She was trying not to picture anyone in particular sitting in the boat with her, when Flint walked past the open window. He had a shovel over one bare shoulder, and he waved as he walked through her line of vision. The sun had warmed the day to a pleasant temperature, and Flint's chest had already grown damp with perspiration. He worked hard, Rani told herself, tapping the end of her pen against the table where she sat. You had to say that much for the man. Whatever else he did, he didn't shirk the rough work his job required. The Andersons were getting their money's worth.

Rani sat staring thoughtfully out the window after Flint had passed. She had never pictured herself as the Lady Chatterley type. She didn't intend to fall for a handyman-gardener. A woman had to take enough risks with men in the world as it was. There was no point deliberately compounding those risks by getting involved with a man who had no clear-cut past and an even less well-defined future.

On the other hand, she thought, I'm only going to be here for another three weeks. That wasn't long enough to get truly involved if one was careful, was it? A real relationship took time and effort. She intended putting neither into her association with Flint Cottrell.

Involved relationship or not, three weeks is long enough to find yourself in bed with him if you aren't careful, she warned herself grimly. But if she were cautious, she might be able to walk the fine line between friendship and an affair. And a part of her wanted to be friends with Cottrell, even though he could easily annoy her. It was a matter of maintaining control of the situation, Rani decided as she got to her feet. She could do it.

"Flint?" She stepped outside into the sunlight and looked around for him. When he didn't answer, she shoved her fingers into the back pockets of her jeans and walked to the side of the cottage where the broken brick path was. Flint was on his knees in the dirt, prying loose a brick. There was a stack of old dirt-covered red bricks beside him. Rani looked down, noticing how the light disappeared into the depths of his thick, dark hair. "What are you doing?"

"What does it look like I'm doing?"

"Handymen aren't supposed to be flippant with their betters," she drawled. "You're going to have to work on the proper attitude of meek deference."

He looked up at that, green eyes narrowing against the sun. "Deference?"

"Yes, deference. Know what it means?"

"I'll look it up this evening."

"You do that. I came out here to ask you if you wanted to go boating with me tomorrow afternoon."

He rocked back on his haunches, dusting off his hands. "Does this mean I'm forgiven for playing the heavy-handed lover last night?"

"The role isn't yours to play, is it?" she retorted.

"I'd like to go boating with you," he answered, paying no attention to her comment. "What are we going to do for a boat?"

"They rent rowboats and outboards down by the lake."

His mouth curved faintly. "Can you row?"

"The reason I'm inviting you along is so that you can do that part," she answered sweetly. "You're the handyman around here."

"Yes, ma'am. I'd be pleased to row my lady's boat." He tugged at an imaginary cap and smiled ingratiatingly.

Rani groaned. "I don't think you're ever going to be any good at it."

"Deference?"

"Yes, deference. And here I was going to pack a picnic lunch and everything."

"I promise to get real good at exhibiting deference if you promise to pack a picnic lunch. I can't even remember the last time I had a picnic lunch. Ants and all?"

"I was hoping to skip the ants." She smiled down at him, and Flint grinned back.

"It's a deal."

She nodded, pleased. "I called Dewhurst this morning," Rani added on a softer note.

"Dewhurst?"

"The man who originally appraised this ring for me." She held out her hand. "He reassured me that it was definitely fake."

Flint shrugged, looking unconcerned. "It's a little large to be real, I suppose."

"He also said the setting isn't more than a hundred years old, if that. So there goes your theory of this being the ring that belongs in your legend."

"He's wrong about that." Flint went back to work on the brick path. "Ambrose was sure of the setting's history. He might have replaced the real emerald with a fake, but he wouldn't have messed with the setting."

"I don't think Mr. Dewhurst would make that kind of mistake, Flint," Rani stated firmly. "Perhaps this isn't the same ring that was originally in my uncle's collection. Have you thought of that?"

"It's the same one Ambrose showed me a year and a half ago."

"But, Flint, it's just not as old as it would have to be to fit your legend. Why do you have to be so stubborn? Can't you just accept the fact that the whole thing is a fake?"

"No."

Rani exhaled with a groan of disgust. "Stubborn, hard-headed man. Do you come from a long line of mules?"

"I doubt it. Mules are sterile, aren't they? They don't breed."

"Details," she snapped. "I'm speaking in general terms. Why are you so dead set on believing this is the ring that belongs to your legend?"

He stopped work on the path again. "I've done a lot of research on that ring, Rani. I know that at least the setting is for real. Want to hear some of the stories that go with it?"

"I'm not sure," she hedged.

"They're very romantic."

She hesitated and then nodded, "Well, in that case, tell them to me."

Five

I think I'm going to need a beer to help me get through these stories." Flint got to his feet. "Besides, I deserve a break. Want one?"

"A break or a beer?"

"A beer," Flint confirmed dryly, starting toward the cottage. "You're already on a month-long break. Do you do this every winter?"

"Take so much time off? No. I told you I had some unused vacation from last year and I had to take it or lose it. To tell you the truth, I was just thinking this morning that I was getting a little bored. I thought a nice long, relaxing rest in the mountains sounded wonderful, but as it turns out I think I should have opted for something more exciting. Like Club Med."

Flint laughed. Rani realized it was the first time she had heard him truly laugh. It was a full, hearty sound that came from deep in his chest. She decided as she trotted after him that she liked it. He ought to laugh more often.

"What's the matter?" she challenged. "Don't you see me as the Club Med type?"

"I'm not sure what the Club Med type is," he hedged, opening the door of the cottage.

"I'm not sure either, but I know what the image is." Rani waited on the step while he collected the beers from the refrigerator.

"Sexy?" he asked as he came back outside. He popped the top on a cold can and handed it to her. Green eyes moved consideringly over her from head to toe. "You'd qualify on that basis, I think. You're not the centerfold type, but there's something about you that makes a man know you'd feel good in his hands. Something soft and warm and lively."

Rani nearly choked on her beer. "Lively! Lively?"

"Yeah, you know." Flint waved his hand in a vain attempt to collect the right word. "*Lively*. Exciting. Responsive. Enthusiastic. Eager."

"Oh, lord." Rani sat down on one of the folding chairs Flint had set on the lawn in front of the cottage. "Forget lively. Next time I want to know what a man thinks of me I'll hand him a thesaurus first."

"I've already got one," Flint told her. "I looked you up in it last night. That's how I came up with lively."

Rani felt the heat in her face and tried to extinguish it with another swallow of cold beer. It was definitely time to get the conversation back under control. She seemed to spend a great deal of time keeping Flint under control. "About these stories you said you were going to tell me," she prompted firmly.

He shrugged, the smooth muscles of his bare, tanned shoulders moving easily as he took the second chair and stretched out his legs. Sitting there with a beer in his hand, his jeans scruffy and stained and his hair awry, he looked exactly what he said he was: a hardworking man who was taking a temporary break. Rani stared at him from beneath her lashes wondering why her intuition was telling her that Flint Cottrell would never fit neatly into a single category. It would be easier if he did, she thought. She'd like to be able to pigeonhole him so that she could feel more in command of the relationship between them. It wasn't going to be easy. It was hard to categorize and forget a man who had spent his life chasing legends.

"The first story takes place in the seventeen hundreds. That's when the Clayborne ring first appeared. It was given to the eldest daughter of a very wealthy English lord. She was wearing it one evening when her coach was held up by a highwayman."

"How exciting."

"The truth is it was rather dangerous. The lady and her chaperon were terrified. The highwayman was in the process of stealing their valuables when another highwayman appeared. The second man sent the first one packing."

Rani smiled. "And then took milady's jewels himself?"

"Nope. The second highwayman is our hero. He nobly apologized to the lady for the poor manners of some of his brethren on the road and then he stole a kiss."

"Only a kiss?" Rani asked skeptically.

"According to the story. At any rate, the Clayborne lady was exceedingly grateful. She was allowed to proceed on her way. But the next evening she met the highwayman who had rescued her. She recognized him at once, even though he was introduced as Lord Creighton, a new neighbor."

"How did she know who he was? Hadn't he worn a mask that night?"

"She just knew, although she kept the secret to herself."
Flint shrugged. "The thing was, she was furious at the deception. She had been dreaming of a romantic highwayman only to discover he was just a staid neighbor who had inherited the next-door estate. Creighton realized he was in trouble and tried desperately to redeem himself. After having kissed the lady, he was well and truly under the spell of her ring, according to the tale. He would do anything for her. He was the perfect gentleman until he realized it wasn't going to get him anywhere. Then he took desperate measures. He dressed up in his highwayman's costume again one dark night and waylaid the lady's coach. This time he took more than a kiss. He took the lady herself and kept her overnight on his estate. The next morning, of course, she had no choice but to marry him. Her family insisted."

"Compromised," Rani said sadly.

"Things were simpler in those days."

"I suppose the punch line is that they eventually lived quite happily together?"

"How did you guess?" Flint tilted the beer can for another swallow. "Milady fell passionately in love with her fake highwayman."

"What was he doing playing at being a highwayman in the first place?"

Flint grinned. "That part of the story isn't clear. From what I can learn it appears there's every likelihood Lord Creighton was a real highwayman, but that he gave up the dangerous game as soon as he realized he was in love."

"Let's hear another story."

"The next one is about Robert and Sara, and it's the best documented."

"When did they live?" Rani asked curiously.

"Early eighteen hundreds. During the Regency period in England. Sara was the daughter of an aristocratic family.

She received the ring on her eighteenth birthday. According to the story, she was a very beautiful, very well-bred young lady. Her family not only had money but a title.''

"Ah-hah. Making her a prize on the marriage market.''

Flint's mouth curved upward briefly. "A very valuable prize. She made quite a splash when she was introduced to society, and the offers for her hand came pouring in during the course of her eighteenth year. From all accounts, Sara enjoyed her status and the situation thoroughly.''

"Good for her,'' Rani cheered.

"She was spoiled.''

"So what?'' Rani sipped her beer.

"She had a fiery temper. She was quite capable of cutting a man dead at a ball if he annoyed her. She was proud and probably quite vain and much too independent to her family's way of thinking.''

Rani raised her beer in salute to the distant Sara. "Attagirl, Sara.''

Flint eyed her speculatively. "Why do I get the feeling you're already taking sides in this story?''

"Because I am.''

"Yeah, well, Sara met her match when she was introduced to Robert.''

"Who was Robert?''

"A brash young sea captain from Boston. He was in England to settle the estate of a distant relative. While he was there he met Sara and immediately fell for her. Sara apparently found him quite a novelty. An amusing change from the soft, pampered males she was accustomed to seeing in society. She turned on the charm, and presumably the ring, and Robert was soon dancing at the end of her string. Apparently she got a kick out of shocking her parents and friends by being seen with him at some of the best social functions.''

"A lady has to take her pleasures where she can," Rani said commiseratingly.

Flint frowned. "Sara found Robert amusing and useful for causing all sorts of interesting commotion, but she was very much aware of her status. She had no intention of going too far and finding herself compromised."

"There's that word again. Compromised," Rani repeated thoughtfully. "An outmoded word. No longer applicable in today's society."

"Well, it was still applicable back then. Sara knew perfectly well she might have been obliged to marry Robert if she went too far in her fun and games. So she kept things under control."

"With the aid of the ring?"

Flint exhaled slowly. "So the story goes. Who knows? At any rate, Sara kept Robert dancing at a discreet distance, close enough to tantalize him, but not so close that she would find herself in an untenable situation."

"Robert tolerated this treatment?"

"Until Livermore appeared on the scene."

Rani smiled. "Who's Livermore?"

"A gentleman with a title as good as the one held by Sara's family. He decided Sara would make the perfect bride. Her family was ready to marry off Sara, and Lord Livermore looked like a viable candidate as a husband for their daughter. The perfect match."

"How did Sara feel about all this?"

"Oh, she agreed with her family. It was an excellent match. Livermore was reasonably good-looking and in the right age bracket. He had good estates and lots of horses. Sara was very fond of hunting. She was quite happy with the marriage proposal and was on the verge of accepting it when the truth came to light. Lord Livermore was virtually bankrupt. He wanted Sara for her money."

"Where was Robert while all this was going on?" Rani asked.

"The poor guy was trying to convince Sara to forget her grand marriage plans and run off to America with him, of course. Sara found the idea laughable. She had no intention of banishing herself to the uncivilized wilds of North America, even though she was very attracted to Robert."

"A woman has to look after her own future. Robert undoubtedly appeared to be a high risk."

"Undoubtedly," Flint agreed neutrally. "Well, things got messy when Sara's family turned down Lord Livermore's marriage proposal. He arranged to kidnap Sara and hold her for a few days at his hunting lodge in Scotland."

"After which," Rani said knowledgeably, "she would have found herself thoroughly compromised and more or less obliged to marry the evil lord."

"Exactly. Enter our hero, Robert, to the rescue. He discovered Livermore's plans at the last minute and raced off to rescue Sara. He caught up with the coach, which was on its way to the border, fought a duel with Lord Livermore and rescued Sara. Robert had her safely delivered back into her family's hands before morning. Her honor was saved."

"What about Livermore?" Rani demanded.

"He spent several weeks recovering from his wounds."

"Oh. In other words, he was out of the picture. Did Sara fall madly in love with the brave Robert?"

"Not quite. Robert made the tactical mistake of telling Sara exactly what he thought of her high-handed, arrogant manners during the trip back to her family's home the night he rescued her. He was rather blunt about it and implied she was a selfish, spoiled young lady who needed a firm hand on the reins."

"Uh-oh. I'll bet Robert then went on to tell her he was just the man to bring her into line, right?"

"How did you guess?"

"I could see it coming," Rani sighed. "Stupid of Robert. There the poor woman is, probably terrified at having barely escaped being kidnapped, still in shock from having witnessed a bloody duel. She's thoroughly traumatized and then this rude upstart from America starts in on a lecture. I'm sure Robert wasn't her idea of a hero."

"Apparently not, because although her family was extremely grateful for her safe return, Sara refused to see Robert after that. But Robert, poor soul, was very much in love with her."

Rani waved that aside. "Then he shouldn't have yelled at her."

Flint's gaze narrowed. "She deserved it."

"Now who's taking sides in this story?"

Flint took a long swallow of beer before continuing. "Moving right along..."

"Yes, let's."

He shot her a quelling look. "As I said, Robert was still desperately in love. Given the fact that Sara was treating him badly and had all along, we have to assume he was under the spell of the ring."

"That's one explanation," Rani agreed blithely.

"But after the rescue, Sara pushed Robert a little too far. When she refused to see him, he decided he had to do something drastic. So he kidnapped her."

Rani was startled. "Another kidnapping? Just like the hero did in the first story? I think I see a pattern developing here."

"You're right. Robert made his way into Sara's bedroom, wrapped her up in a blanket and carried her off one night."

"Good grief! He thought that was going to make her look on him more favorably?"

"He thought," Flint stated bluntly, "that it would leave her with no other choice but to marry him."

"He deliberately compromised her! Just like the first guy did to the Clayborne lady, and the evil Lord Livermore tried to do." Rani was incensed.

"It probably seemed the simplest approach under the circumstances."

"It was despicable."

"Yeah, well, whatever, it worked. The next morning a very subdued young Sara married him under a special license. Her family had no choice but to accept the situation. Sara and Robert left for America a month later."

"Poor Sara! What happened to her?"

Flint grinned. "She raised six kids and captivated Boston society. Everyone said she was a fine example of the perfect wife. Loving, obedient and fertile. Just as the lady in the first story had been. The ladies who own the rings make excellent wives."

"And Robert?"

"Robert is said to have been a very satisfied husband. He was wildly in love with his wife and she with him for the rest of their lives."

"So Sara fell in love with him after all, hmmm?" Rani thought about that.

"Once Robert had taken her to bed, she didn't have any choice. According to the legend of the ring, she was then as ensnared as he was."

Rani frowned. "Do you think he raped her that night he kidnapped her? Was that how he subdued her?"

Flint scowled and tipped his beer can to his mouth. "No, I don't think he raped her. He seduced her."

"Hah. That's your interpretation."

"The few people who saw Sara the morning after the kidnapping said she was quieter than usual but not at all unhappy. In fact, it was said she was the image of the happy, blushing bride."

"Amazing how a legend can smooth over some of the facts." Rani remarked. "Are you going to straighten things out when you write these stories? After all, you're the one who's going to force the truth down everybody's throat, right?"

"Facts are facts. I'm not going to change the verifiable details of the tales. In the case of the story of Sara and Robert, I'll simply point out that their marriage undoubtedly came about because a temperamental young woman pushed a passionate young man a little too far. The first story involves a similar situation. Both men lost their patience and took advantage of the conventions of the times to force the ladies into marriage. There was no magic involved."

"Just passion?"

Flint smiled. "Don't you think that's sufficient explanation?"

"Do you? You seem very ambivalent about this ring, Flint. Sometimes you scoff at it and other times I get the impression you half believe in it."

He tilted his head, studying her intently in the sunlight. "Maybe you'd better hope I don't buy the legends as fact."

Rani felt chilled. Much of the companionable warmth that had enveloped her as she listened to Flint's tales evaporated. "Why is that?" she asked softly.

"Because if I decide the legend is for real, I might decide to put it to the test. I might seduce you the way those other two men seduced their ladies. If the tales about the ring are valid, you'd be helpless to resist me then, wouldn't you? You'd be bound to me."

Rani felt caught, trapped in a glistening, silky web that made it impossible to get out of the chair and stalk off toward the house. The sunlight was suddenly too strong, causing everything around her to become too sharp and clear and full of color. The green of Flint's eyes, for example, was now far too vivid. She remembered what Charles Dewhurst had said about true emeralds. There was a fire trapped within them, green flames that mesmerized whoever looked too deeply. In that instant, Rani knew, she had looked far too deeply into living emeralds.

"Rani?"

She blinked, struggling to break free of the odd, trapped sensation she was experiencing. "What would you do to me if I were bound to you?" she heard herself ask.

"Make love to you often and well." He spoke as though he had already considered the question and had long since decided on an answer.

Rani felt strangely breathless. She must get away from him, but she still couldn't move. "Until your next handyman or gardening job took you to another state or another country? Or until another, more interesting woman came along?"

He smiled faintly. "You forget the ring works both ways. I'd be just as trapped as I was before I made love to you. The only difference is that after I've seduced you, you'll no longer have the privilege of being in charge. You won't be able to keep me dancing at the end of the string."

"I don't see much evidence of your dancing now!"

"Think not? Look at how easily you handle me."

Rani flushed. "I hadn't noticed."

"You tell me when and how to write, imply I'm shiftless and unstable—"

"I never said shiftless!"

"You chew me up one side and down the other just for being in your kitchen when you bring home your date—"

Rani was incensed now. "You deserved that."

GET 4 FREE BOOKS, FREE FOLDING UMBRELLA, FREE MYSTERY GIFT!

TO ENTER: Fill out, detach below, and affix postage. See back pages of books for OFFICIAL SWEEPSTAKES INFORMATION and mail your entry before deadline date shown in rules.

S ♥ I ♥ L ♥ H ♥ O ♥ U ♥ E ♥ T ♥ T ♥ E

LUCKY HEARTS

SWEEPSTAKES

Free prizes— you must enter to win. Detach here and mail today!

*Sweeps entry—
process immediately!*

Silhouette Books®

Prize Headquarters
120 Brighton Road
P.O. Box 5084
Clifton, NJ 07015-5084

"You only let me kiss you when you want to be kissed and you call it off when you want to stop."

Rani's mouth tightened. "It's a woman's prerogative."

"You assume I'm available when you get bored and want someone to row a boat for you," Flint continued blandly.

"That's not true. I invited you along because I thought you might enjoy the outing."

"You've made it clear that, as a lover, you think I'd be a high risk."

"Well, you would."

"And you've also made it clear you're a lady who doesn't take risks. That's not very good for my self-esteem."

"I didn't realize your self-esteem needed to be pampered," Rani snapped. She finally managed to get to her feet. "Look, if you don't want to go out on the lake, just say so. I thought you'd appreciate the break, but I guess I was wrong. Thanks for the story hour. I don't think I want to hear any more Clayborne ring stories today." In her agitation she clutched the empty beer can. There was a crunching sound, and she looked down in astonishment to see the can crumpled between her fingers.

"Don't get the idea you've turned into Wonder Woman," Flint advised with a faint grin. "Anyone can do that with an aluminum beer can."

"I'll remember that." Rani tossed the can in his direction. He plucked it easily out of the air as she turned to stride toward the back door of her cottage.

"Rani," he called after her. "What time tomorrow are we going to the lake?"

She swung around to glare at him, her hand on the doorknob. "This is not a good time to ask me. I am seriously considering withdrawing the invitation."

Flint shook his head in mild reproach. "You're playing with fire. You know that, don't you?"

Rani stepped into the house and let the door slam shut behind her. She was playing with fire, all right. Emerald-green fire. The flames were licking at her heels.

By three o'clock that afternoon, Rani was too restless to convince herself any longer that she was simply enjoying a quiet day around the house. She had to get out. Perhaps she would walk over to the lake and throw stones or something equally exhilarating. Anything to get away from the feeling of being surrounded by Flint Cottrell's presence.

Even as she came to that conclusion, he opened her front door without bothering to knock. He stood on the threshold, wiping his damp forehead with the back of his bare arm.

"I'm going to have to run into town to pick up a few things at the hardware store. Want to come along?" he asked.

"No thanks," Rani said, aware that she sounded waspish.

"Okay. Suit yourself. I'll be back in a half hour or forty-five minutes."

Rani moved over to the window to watch as Flint slid into the black Jeep and turned the key in the ignition. He was gone before she could think of a graceful way of changing her mind. Just as well, she told herself. She didn't want to give him the wrong impression. He already had enough misconceptions about their association.

She prowled restlessly around the cottage, looking for something to take the edge off her uneasiness. She walked out into the garden and examined Flint's work. He really did have a knack for this sort of thing, she admitted to herself. It was obvious he took a deep pleasure in what he did. Sitting on the back steps, chin in hand, Rani contemplated the changes Flint had already made in the chaotic yard. Bushes had been trimmed, plants pruned for winter, grass raked. An orderly atmosphere was being gently established here. It made Rani even more nervous suddenly. She got to her feet, dusted her hands and decided to take a walk to the lake.

Zipp meowed at her feet as she opened the door and urged him into the house. Rani glanced down. "No, you can't come with me. I'm going over to the lake and you might get lost."

Zipp looked distinctly scornful of the possibility. He jumped onto the windowsill to watch forlornly as Rani headed off across the road. She turned to wave once to him and then set about making a serious effort to enjoy herself. She wasn't going to let flint Cottrell influence her whole vacation with his tales of the ring or with his purely masculine interest in acquiring a convenient bed partner for the remainder of her vacation.

That was what he was after, of course. A bed partner. It was the only answer that made sense. He was the kind of man who would be gone on the next breath of wind. Furthermore, he didn't come from her world. He didn't even come from a world with which she was vaguely familiar. He was a restless wanderer, a man who chased legends for a hobby and who made his living by doing whatever came to hand. It wouldn't surprise her to learn that some of the things that had come to hand in the course of his life had been less than respectable. He hadn't gotten that scar on his shoulder while gardening.

Rani crossed the road and started into a stand of fir and pine. The needles were occasionally slippery underfoot, and she had to use some caution on the long, gentle slope down toward the water. Rani knew from a previous walk that the hike would take about fifteen or twenty minutes. Through breaks in the forest she caught glimpses of the lake shining in the bright sun. Here in the trees the light was pleasantly dappled and golden. She began to relax. Taking the walk had been a good idea. She realized that she was going to have to organize more outings for herself, however. She wasn't the type to simply sit around and relax for several weeks. It had seemed like such a good idea at the time, but the reality was proving to be full of complications.

Rani made a firm decision not to involve Flint in any of her plans. She wouldn't have him accusing her of using him as a convenient companion or a source of entertainment. She frowned to herself, annoyed at the way he'd interpreted her invitation to go boating. She would ask Mike Slater instead. It occurred to her that Flint would probably interpret that action as spiteful and juvenile. She was stuck, regardless of what she did. Maybe she'd just go out by herself.

There were several cabins along the shoreline of the lake. The woods were safe through here, even during hunting season. The area was posted, and any sane hunter would know better than to risk coming so close to a populated region. Rani paused for a while to study some pinecones that had fallen. She knew people who did remarkable things in the way of Christmas decorations with pinecones. With a sigh, she decided she wasn't one of them. She couldn't really see herself making a wreath out of them or gilding one with gold paint. She just wasn't the type.

What type was she? Rani stood still for a while under the dappled, shadowed trees and wondered about that. She had been very sure for a long time now that she knew exactly what sort of woman she was, what she wanted out of life and what kind of relationships she sought. She had been in control of herself and her environment for several years. Ever since college she'd become increasingly independent and content with the safe, careful world she had created.

Her home in Santa Rosa, one of the pleasant towns just north of San Francisco, was cozy and comfortable, every inch of it done to her personal satisfaction. She hadn't had to consult anyone else's opinion. She liked her job at the public library where she was in charge of the reference department at one of the branches. Her social life was as full as she wanted it to be, no more, no less. The men she dated were never allowed too close. They were pleasant companions or interesting dinner dates drawn from her circle of college-educated, upscale friends. The various points of reference in her universe orbited around her in neat, predictable paths, and she was always in control of those paths. The possibility that such neatness and controlled predictability had meant she'd steered clear of violent passion or outrageous risks bothered her not at all.

At least it hadn't bothered her until a man with emerald eyes had appeared on her doorstep and demanded entrance into her life. Now Rani found herself silently having to defend the way of life she had created. She shouldn't have to justify her decisions. She'd made them with intelligence and a clear knowledge of what she wanted and needed. The restlessness she was feeling today bothered her. She knew deep down it didn't stem from boredom.

She was considering the ramifications of what was happening to her when she slid on a patch of pine needles. She lost her balance, clutched wildly at a low branch and sat down with awkward heaviness, just as the fierce crack of a rifle shot echoed through the trees.

"Hey, you with the gun," she yelled blindly, staying on the ground. "There are people around here. This isn't hunting land."

There was no response. Rani was more shaken by the proximity of the shot than she wanted to admit. It was still quite far to the safety of the lakeshore and there was little in the way of civilization between here and her cottage. She decided to stay put until she was certain the hunter had realized his mistake and departed. He was probably as startled by her shout as she had been by his shot.

But even as she lay on her stomach, hugging the ground behind a wide fir, another shot split the still air. The second shot left her not only angry but scared and puzzled. Perhaps the hunter hadn't heard her yell. The sound of a rifle shot probably carried a good deal farther than a human voice. Some fool hunter had probably caught sight of her movement through his field glasses and had fired without making certain she was a deer. She ought to have worn her red sweater instead of the black one with the yellow sunburst embroidered on it. Rani decided to try another yell.

"Whoever you are with the gun, I am not a deer, understand? You're shooting on posted land." She waited for a response. There was none. It occurred to Rani that she ought to move herself from the vicinity.

Very cautiously she began inching her way back to the cottage. Not daring to raise herself too far off the ground, she crawled painfully over needles and small pebbles. There was silence for a while, and she began to hope that the stray hunter had finally realized his mistake.

She was almost at the top of the gently sloping hillside when she saw Zipp. He came trotting into view looking extremely purposeful, as if he knew exactly where he was going.

"Zipp! For Pete's sake, what are you doing here? I told you to stay at home." Rani started to sit up and reach for the cat when a third shot rang out. The hunter was following her. Rani gasped, clutched Zipp and started to yell again. She was very scared now. But before she could try another warning call, Flint's voice cracked through the gloom, low and sharp with command.

"Stay down."

Startled, Rani turned her head to see him slithering over the rise to join her. He came around the side of a fir tree with all the easy skill of a man who has more than once clung to the ground while under fire. She didn't see the blue steel pistol in his fist until he raised his hand to aim it past his shoulder.

"My God, Flint, what are you doing?"

The pistol barked furiously in the dappled silence. Zipp jumped nervously in Rani's grasp. Before the echo of the first shot had died away, Flint squeezed off another. Belatedly, Rani realized he wasn't aiming high in warning. He was shooting at the level a man would be standing. Rani saw the coldly savage expression in his face as he waited, gun in hand, for the hunter's response.

Silence descended on the woods. For a very long time Flint said nothing, his full attention on his surroundings. Beside him, Rani sat motionless. She shivered, thinking of what might have happened. But she shuddered even more when she stared at the weapon held so expertly in Flint's fist. Her eyes went mutely from the gun to his green gaze. Cold green fire. She had never seen anything so cold.

"Are you all right?" he asked quietly.

"Yes." She paused to dampen her lips. "Yes, I'm fine. Just a little shaken. How did you . . . ?"

"I got back from town and found you gone but your car was still in the drive. I figured you'd decided to take a walk, and since the lake is the only place anyone would walk to around here, I started after you. Zipp wanted to come along. He knew exactly where you'd gone."

"But the gun," she protested weakly.

"I keep it around as a security blanket," he said dryly, getting slowly to his feet. "Come on, I think we're safe enough now. Let's get back to the house."

Rani wanted to ask him why he had brought the pistol with him when he'd followed her into the woods. She wanted to know why he'd aimed low instead of firing a warning shot in the hunter's direction. She wanted to know why Flint kept a gun as a security blanket. A hundred questions hovered on her lips.

But Rani said nothing as she held Zipp tightly under one arm and allowed Flint to take her free hand to lead her quickly back through the woods toward her cottage.

Six

"Stupid hunters," Rani muttered as she stepped gratefully into the security of her cottage. She plopped Zipp down on the floor and turned to face Flint. He had been surprisingly quiet on the trip back through the woods. "We should report this incident to the sheriff, not that it'll do much good. By the time anyone gets around to investigating, whoever was doing the shooting will be long gone. After those shots you fired, he must have realized he had come too close to something that wasn't a deer."

"I'll give the sheriff a call," Flint said quietly. He reached for the phone. "Why don't you go clean up?"

Rani looked down at her dusty clothing. She had pine needles stuck in her sweater and a few more in her hair. "Good idea. Tell him that those shots were awfully close. One of them broke off a piece of bark on the tree beside me. If I hadn't slipped on some needles at the right moment, I might have been hit."

Flint's face was very lean and hard, devoid of almost all expression. But Rani sensed the fierceness in him, saw it glowing in the emerald of his eyes. When she glanced up and caught his gaze, she felt an uneasy twinge. It overrode some of the relief she had been experiencing. Remembering the gun, she looked around for it. Flint had set it down on the end table that held the phone. Rani wasn't quite certain what to say about it. One of her many rules in life was not to get involved with men who were interested in firearms. Of course, she reminded herself, she was hardly *involved* with Flint Cottrell.

"You shouldn't have gone for a walk in the woods during hunting season, Rani."

"I was only going over to the lake. That's hardly open hunting land. There are cabins all around this part of the woods. Hunters aren't supposed to be anywhere near them."

"You've said yourself, they aren't always careful or law-abiding." Flint was dialing a number he'd found in the front of the small local phone book. "You should have stuck around here until I got back. I had no idea you were planning on going for a walk. We could have driven to the lake."

"Flint, this has been a very unsettling experience, to say the least. I would appreciate a little understanding here. I have never been shot at in my life. I could have been killed out there."

"Yes," he agreed, waiting for the phone to ring on the other end.

"So why are you lecturing me?" she demanded. "I need sympathy, not a lecture. For heaven's sake, I wasn't doing anything wrong or even particularly reckless. The short distance between here and the lake is posted land and should be perfectly safe."

"I'll see what I can come up with in the way of sympathy and understanding while you're taking a shower and changing your clothes. I might be a little short on both for a while. I'm still using what sympathy and understanding I've got on myself. You gave me one hell of a scare, lady." He broke off to answer the greeting on the other end.

Rani glowered at him for a moment as she listened to the succinct, factual report of the shooting incident. From the way he handled it, a person could get the impression Cottrell had handled this sort of thing before. Rani groaned and headed for the bathroom. It was irritating to have to admit it, but Flint did have a point. She knew one had to take precautions during hunting season. It just had never occurred to her that the walk from her cottage to the lake would be a dangerous one.

It was almost dusk when Rani emerged from a lengthy shower and pulled on a fresh pair of jeans and a bright orange shirt that was patterned with a thin black stripe. She fluffed up her hair, coiling it into a knot at the back of her head and then paused to examine herself in the mirror. She looked normal enough, but she wasn't feeling normal.

The restlessness she had felt earlier in the day had turned into a definite feeling of uneasiness. Perhaps the jolt she had received from having a careless hunter take potshots at her had produced a kind of shock to her system. It certainly wasn't the sort of incident one got over in a hurry.

Zipp sat on the bed behind her, watching her through half-shut eyes. Rani turned around to scratch his ears. "You were a hero today, Zipp. Did you realize that? Tracked me down through the woods like a smart hunting dog. Sorry, no offense."

Zipp's purring engine rumbled into full throttle. Rani watched him for a moment as he sprawled contentedly on the bed while she thought about her other rescuing hero. Flint hadn't quite matched up to her inner image of a hero, although she had to admit he had arrived on the scene with excellent timing. Timing was undoubtedly a major factor in that sort of thing. In all her safe, prosaic life Rani had never before gotten herself into a situation from which she needed rescuing. She wondered at her odd reaction.

Maybe it was the sight of the gun Flint had been carrying when he'd shown up out there in the woods that had upset her. Here she was complaining about all the hunters on the loose in the vicinity without even being aware that her nearest neighbor had a very ugly weapon of his own. Rani knew enough about guns to know that handguns did not come under the heading of sporting equipment. Handguns were designed with only one purpose in mind. That purpose wasn't shooting deer.

Something else was bothering her, too. There had been a quietness about Flint when he'd found her in the woods. A lethal, efficient, competent quietness that she only now acknowledged. It had seemed to come from deep within him, and it hadn't faded much when they'd reached the safety of the house. Rani stood gazing out her window into the garden, absently stroking Zipp. It was Flint's unnatural inner stillness that was causing part of her feeling of unease. Rescuing heroes were supposed to sweep you into their arms and offer comfort and soothing sympathy. Rani didn't think she was likely to get very much of that from Flint. Perhaps it was just as well. She wasn't quite sure how she would react if Flint ever took her in his arms and offered real comfort.

The clatter of glasses being taken from the kitchen cupboard jerked her attention back to the moment. Rani sighed, stopped petting Zipp and headed down the hall to the kitchen. Aware that the free stroking was over for the moment, Zipp bounded off the bed and followed.

"Want a drink?" Flint inquired calmly as Rani appeared in the doorway. "Personally, I need one." He was already pouring himself a glass of amber liquid.

"Where did you get the whiskey?" Rani asked, more for something to say than anything else. She just couldn't quite figure out how to take Flint Cottrell, she realized.

"Picked it up in town after I went to the hardware store."

"Oh. I think I'd rather have a glass of wine."

"Suit yourself." He opened the refrigerator and pulled out a bottle of Chemin Blanc that Rani had been chilling. "How are you feeling? Still shaky?"

Rani began to relax a little, coming to the conclusion that Flint was now genuinely concerned about her emotional state. "Not really. But I feel a bit strange. I guess near misses affect a lot of people that way."

"Ummm." He removed the cork efficiently and poured wine into a glass. Vaguely Rani recalled that he'd once tended bar in some far-off corner of the world.

"You, uh, been around a lot of near misses in the course of your career as a handyman-gardener, Flint?" She hadn't intended to ask such a provocative question, but as he put the cold glass of wine in her hand, Rani couldn't seem to stop herself. Something about him made her want to goad and provoke a little. She was beginning to realize she wanted some answers about this man.

"A few." He leaned back against the sink and sipped the neat whiskey. His steady green gaze rested on her face. "The sheriff said he'd send someone out to scout the area where the shots were fired but warned us not to expect anything. Whoever was hunting out there will be long gone by now."

"Especially after having taken return fire from the 'deer' he thought was going to be such an easy target. I'm sure you put a scare into whoever it was, Flint."

"You looked more than a little scared yourself when I found you. I'm glad you had the sense to get down and stay down."

"It came naturally after the first shot went overhead," she retorted.

"Yeah, I guess it would. Don't go for any more solitary hikes again, Rani."

She slanted him a half-resentful glance. "I don't need the lectures, Flint. I've told you that. If it's any consolation, you don't have to worry. I won't be running around in the woods until after hunting season is over."

"Poor Rani. You're not used to getting lectures, are you?"

"Nope." She smiled suddenly. "But I do know how to say thank you. I do owe you my thanks. I was very glad to see you coming through the trees this afternoon, Flint." She put down her glass and stepped toward him. He didn't move as she stood on tiptoe to brush her mouth against his.

"You always say thanks like that?"

Rani flushed slightly, moving away. She didn't understand his reaction. She'd assumed he'd appreciate the small kiss. "Sorry, I didn't mean to insult you. Would you prefer a check instead? For services rendered? I believe you told me that you'd done some bodyguarding during your career as a handyman. I'm willing to pay for professional expertise."

"Stop it, Rani."

"Stop what? I don't know how to handle you, Flint. You come to my rescue as though you've done that sort of thing a lot. Then you act as if it was mostly my fault that I needed rescuing in the first place. Now you criticize me for trying to express a little gratitude. What is it with you?"

He stared at her for a moment and then muttered something under his breath that she couldn't quite catch. "I told you, you gave me a scare this afternoon."

"I gave myself one, too!"

"I know. I'm feeling a little tense."

"Is that an explanation or an apology?" she asked.

"Just a statement of fact."

"Try some more whiskey," she suggested blandly. "Maybe it'll help."

He shook his head, a reluctant smile catching the edge of his mouth. "I think it's going to take more than a little whiskey. How about you?"

She slowly returned his attempt at a smile. "Speaking for myself, it's going to take at least a second glass. I'm a little tense, too."

"You want some company for dinner?"

"Don't be subtle, Flint. Why don't you come right out and ask to stay for dinner?"

He grinned and took one gliding step forward. He rested his arms on her shoulders, his glass still held in his right hand behind her head. Very slowly he lowered his mouth to kiss her, a slow, lingering, hungry kiss that penetrated all the way to her toes. When he lifted his head, there was a hint of green fire in his eyes.

"May I stay for dinner?"

"Yes," Rani agreed, aware of the huskiness in her voice. "You can stay."

For a moment they stood very still, looking at each other and then, as though satisfied with what he saw in her face, Flint nodded his head once and released her. "I make one of the world's best salad dressings."

"You do?" She watched in amusement as he opened the refrigerator again and started moving items.

"Worked for a guy once who had a French chef. I spent a fair amount of time in the kitchen. Mostly I spent the time eating. The salad dressing was the only thing I really learned how to make."

Rani didn't ask what kind of work Flint had done for the guy who'd had his own French chef.

The dressing was delicious. It went perfectly on the spin-ach-and-mushroom salad. By the time dinner was over, Rani's inner tension had dissolved. So, apparently, had Flint's. He made himself at home in the living room after dinner, sprawling in a chair with Zipp on his lap and talked lazily about the article he was trying to write. Rani sat lis-tening, her feet curled under her and wondered about this most unusual man who had wandered into her life. She felt bemused and amused, fascinated and wary, attracted and cautious. All in all, she simply didn't know what to do with Flint Cottrell.

"I didn't tell you the last story I've documented concern-ing the ring," said Flint.

"Does it follow the pattern of the other two tales?"

"Yeah. Except the lady in this case was the daughter of a wealthy Texas rancher. She got kidnapped and held for ransom by outlaws."

"Was the hero one of the outlaws?"

"No. He was a cowboy with a somewhat shady past who knew how to handle a gun. The lady's father hired him to get his daughter back."

"Which he did, right? And then he proceeded to fall in love with the lady who, of course, spurned him," Rani concluded spiritedly.

"Have you heard this story?"

"No, but I told you, I'm beginning to see a pattern in these Clayborne ring stories of yours. What happened this time, Flint? Did the gunslinging cowboy lose his patience and rekidnap the lady for himself?"

"You *have* heard this story before," he accused.

"No, just a couple of very similar ones. It's a male fan-tasy, you know."

"What is?"

"Women falling in love with their captors."

"These women don't fall in love with just any captors. They don't fall for the bad guys. Just the good guys. Who, according to the legend, are captivated themselves."

"Because of the ring?"

"Or something." Flint smiled cryptically.

"Going to spend your whole life chasing legends, Flint?"

"I've already spent enough time chasing legends. What about you, Rani?" Flint asked suddenly. "Going to work in a library all your life?"

"What's wrong with working in a library?"

"Nothing. Going to get married?"

"Maybe. Maybe not. I don't feel any great urge to marry. Do you?"

He looked thoughtful. "I haven't until now."

"You're almost forty, aren't you?

"Don't remind me."

"If you have successfully resisted marriage this long, you'll probably manage to do it a while longer."

"It's not that I've resisted it, exactly," he said, frowning. "There just hasn't been room in my life for a single, special woman."

"Because you're always on the move? Always chasing legends?"

"That part of my life is ending, Rani."

"How many times have you told yourself that in the past?" she countered gently.

He looked startled. "Not once. This is the first time."

"Don't worry. I'm sure by the time you're finished here, you'll be anxious to move on again."

"Is that why you're so wary of me? Because you're afraid I can't make a long-term commitment? You always play it safe, don't you? You're such a sweet little coward, Rani."

"No," she protested softly. "Just cautious."

He smiled faintly and pushed Zipp off his lap. The cat stalked off to the kitchen to see what was left in his food dish. Flint watched him go and then looked at Rani. "You'll never get rid of that cat, you know. He's with you for the duration."

"He knows a good thing when he's got it."

"So do I, Rani." Flint got to his feet and reached down to tug her up beside him. "So do I."

Rani felt the jumble of emotions within her suddenly begin to swirl together in a dizzying mix. She tried to recover her sense of wariness but found herself getting excited instead. Instinctively she made another grab for self-control only to discover she was clutching desire. It was unsettling. Flint was unsettling.

"Show me you're not a coward," he whispered, wrapping her slowly, inevitably, within his arms. "Thank me again for coming to your rescue today."

"Subtlety is definitely not one of your social skills." But she was smiling up at him, her eyes full of the precarious mixture of emotions she was feeling.

"I'll skip the subtlety and try for honesty." Flint took her mouth with sudden intensity, one strong hand curving around her head to anchor her for the deep kiss.

Rani sucked in a shaky breath and felt the most dangerous of the swirling emotions rise to the surface. Flint's mouth was hard and warm and infinitely exciting. She closed her eyes and gave herself up to the passion that flared between herself and the unpredictable, mysterious man who held her. There was no doubt about the need in him, no question of his desire. Of that much she could be absolutely certain.

Rani's hands settled on Flint's shoulders where she could feel the strength in him. But there was a curious gentleness in the way he held her, a tenderness that took away any fears she might have had. When she parted her lips for him, Flint groaned and eagerly took the offering. He explored her mouth urgently, seeking to know the warmth and promise there. Only when he had drunk his fill did he break off the kiss to taste the skin of her throat.

"Flint." His name was a faint, breathless whisper on her lips as Rani nestled against his shoulder. His leg moved, his thigh pushing deliberately against her. The hardness in him took away what remained of her breath.

"You're trembling, sweetheart." He held her even more tightly, as if to stop the fine tremors that rippled through her. "Don't be afraid of me."

"I'm not," she said simply, unable to explain why she was shaking. The thrilling excitement rushing through her could not be contained. She caught his head between her palms and kissed him with soft fierceness. When she opened her eyes, she found him looking down at her, his gaze so brilliant it almost dazzled her.

"I'll take care of you, Rani. I swear it. I'll take good care of you."

"I believe you." She smiled gently. "But I'm not sure that being taken care of is quite what I need tonight."

He bent his head and delicately nipped at her earlobe. "No? What do you need?"

"Do I have to put it into words?"

"Please," he asked in a dark, husky voice. "I need to hear the words."

She sighed, leaning into him so that she could feel all of his heat and desire. The last of her caution evaporated in the flames of this new, raw emotion. "I need you."

"Ah, Rani, my sweet, Rani." Exultantly he scooped her up into his arms and strode toward the bedroom. Rani clung to him, burying her face against his shoulder, one hand toying with the button of the blue cotton work shirt he wore.

With a conscious act of will, she put all thoughts of past and future out of her head.

The bed lay in darkness, and Flint didn't bother to turn on a light. He settled Rani down on the quilt with infinite care and leaned over her, his hands planted on either side of her. She lay looking up at him, her eyes slumberous, her mouth slightly parted. When she touched the side of his face with her fingertips, Flint turned his head to kiss her palm.

"Trust me, Rani."

"Trust you to do what?" She trailed her fingertips around to the nape of his neck and buried them in the thick darkness of his hair.

"Just trust me." He lowered himself beside her, one leg sprawling heavily across her own as if to pin her to the bed. Slowly he began to undo the buttons of her bright orange shirt.

Rani gasped, her fingers briefly clenching him as the material of her shirt fell aside. He murmured her name in soft wonder as he touched her breast. When she lifted herself against his hand in unconscious need, he found the catch of her bra and released it. A moment later Rani was nude to the waist.

"You feel so good, Rani. How did I ever survive without knowing how good you feel?"

She couldn't answer. The words seemed locked in her throat as the urgency in her body threatened to swamp her senses. He was the one who felt good, she thought dazedly. His rough, callused hands were gentle and tantalizing on her nipples. She was becoming aroused with a speed and intensity that was strange and new. For a woman who had always practiced great caution in her relationships with men, this fiery passion was far more dangerous than deep water or thin ice.

Her own fingers fumbled as she tried to remove his shirt. Flint let her struggle with the buttons, clearly enjoying her trembling touch, but when she had finally freed the last button, he yanked off the garment with obvious impatience. Then he came down on top of her, cushioning himself on her breasts.

"I've been wanting this so long," he breathed, his lips at the pulse in her throat. "All this time and I didn't even realize what I was missing."

"Flint... I, oh, please, Flint." She could not talk, not coherently, not at that moment. She was aching for him, and her need was obvious. He gloried in it, making it plain his only desire was to satisfy the passion he had aroused.

When his fingers slipped the fastening of her jeans and tugged them and her panties down her hips, Rani made no protest. She had no wish to halt the inevitable flow of desire that had been unleashed. She waited while he got rid of the last of his own clothing and caught her breath at the undeniable evidence of his own desire. He was rock hard, his rugged body taut with a passion still barely under control.

Flint's eyes met hers as he came back down beside her. Deliberately he stroked the silky skin of her inner thigh. "You could drive me crazy with wanting. Do you realize that? You have such power over me, sweetheart." His fingers moved wickedly on her, finding the center of her physical sensations with unerring accuracy. Rani cried out softly and heard his muttered groan of response.

In that moment she felt alive with feminine power. It gave her the courage to tease and tantalize. "Afraid of me?" She trailed her fingers over his shoulder and down his side to his hip. "Don't be. I only want to hold you and please you."

His mouth curved faintly in the shadows, and it seemed to Rani that his eyes were flaring with an excitement that should have seemed dangerous to her but was not. "You please me, honey. Never doubt that." He took her arm and wrapped it around his neck, then he slid over her, securing her beneath him.

Rani's eyes widened as she felt the first probing touch at the warm, passion-dewed entrance to her most secret place. He was hard and strong, and when he took her he would be overwhelming. Rani knew that with deep, feminine certainty. She wanted him in a way she had never wanted any other man in her life, and yet she was suddenly aware of a new kind of uncertainty. Some of the wariness returned in that moment. Flint didn't push. He held himself firmly under control, savoring the damp readiness of her as he gently stroked the skin of her shoulder with his tongue.

"You want me, honey," he told her thickly.

"Yes."

"And God knows, I want you. Don't be afraid of me. Please don't ever be afraid of me."

"It's all right, Flint. I'm not afraid." She was trembling again as she waited for him. She wasn't afraid, but there was something else going on, something of which she should be wary. It was useless to try to understand. Everything had gone much too far. What was going to happen, had to happen. There was no way now to call it off or change the course of forces that had been set in motion the moment she had opened her door to the man with the emerald eyes. Rani sighed and tightened her arms around Flint.

Sensing her very private surrender and reading the acceptance in her body, Flint chose that instant to move against her and into her. The melding was slow and thorough. He made sure of that, needing to possess her and be possessed by her on every level. Rani whispered his name far back in her throat as his body locked tightly into hers. He swallowed the soft sounds she made, filling her mouth even as he filled the soft, velvety passage between her warm thighs.

The exultation in him was a heady thing. It played with his senses, sending him zinging and ricocheting until he felt exuberantly disoriented. The world narrowed down to the depths of Rani's bed and the hot, tight depths of her body. Nothing else mattered. Nothing else held any long-term importance. This was what he had sought for so long. The restlessness that had dominated him all of his adult life would finally be calmed.

"Wrap your legs around me. Hold me, Rani. Hold me as tightly as you can."

She obeyed. Flint groaned, tightening with spiraling desire as her legs closed around his hips. She felt so right in his arms. So perfectly right. He knew she was still trying to adjust to him. Her inner tension was both physical and emotional. The last thing he wanted to do was hurt her. Desperately Flint reined in his own white-hot need. He would give her time. It had to be good for her. It must be right for her. That was the most crucial thing. Now that he was in possession, he would make sure she took satisfaction in that possession.

He felt her adjusting to him as her body accepted his. Slowly he began to move, seeking the rhythm that would please her. She responded so beautifully, so completely. He could hardly believe the sweet evidence of her eagerness. She was suddenly very hot and clinging, making small, seductive demands that fed the flames of his own passion. Eagerly Flint surged into her, lifting her with his own hands, letting himself get buried in the tight, fiery depths.

Then he sensed a new kind of tension in Rani. She was clinging to him more tightly than ever, her nails raking his shoulders in an unconscious movement that delighted him. Flint felt the tiny, delicate tremors that started deep within her, waited until she cried out and then, with a final deep thrust he allowed himself to find his own near-violent satisfaction. Dimly he heard his hoarse shout of triumph and pleasure mingling with her soft, breathless cries and then he was sinking heavily back into the depths of the quilt.

Slowly, the world that had begun to shift on its axis the night Rani had opened the door to him settled into a new and stable position. Everything was finally the way it was supposed to be, Flint thought fleetingly as he cradled Rani protectively in his arms. Everything felt right.

"Cold?" he asked as Rani's lashes lifted to reveal a languid expression in the depths of her eyes.

"A little," she admitted.

He smiled and tugged the quilt over both of them. "How's that?"

"Much better."

He waited for her to say something else, and when she didn't, he realized he didn't quite know what to say either. It was as if what had just happened between them was too new and dazzling to put into words. Perhaps it was better not to try. Still, there were things that should be said.

Flint took a breath and touched the corner of Rani's mouth. "I know I'm not exactly what you had in mind," he began carefully.

She lay very still in his arms. "Not exactly what I had in mind for what?"

"I know I don't quite match your inner picture of the ideal man. But I meant what I said earlier, Rani. I'll take care of you."

"You keep saying that. It's as if you feel you have some sense of responsibility for me."

"I do," he informed her simply.

Her brows drew together in a small frown of concern. "That's not true, Flint. You don't owe me anything because of tonight. I'm an adult woman. I know what I'm doing.''

He felt a wave of amusement. "I should hope so.''

"Then why the oversized sense of responsibility?''

"I thought you approved of men who have a sense of responsibility. You like nice, stable types, remember?''

"Are you trying to convince me you're really a nice, stable, responsible type under all that vagabond charm?'' She smiled up at him and tugged at a lock of his hair that had fallen over his forehead.

"I didn't know you thought I had much at all in the way of charm.'' He wasn't sure "vagabond charm" was a compliment.

She grinned playfully. "If you didn't have your own peculiar brand of charm, I wouldn't be lying here right now, would I?''

In spite of his need to be serious, Flint found himself responding to the teasing quality that was bubbling through her. He discovered he liked it when she teased him. It was a rare sort of intimacy for him, and he found he thoroughly enjoyed it. "Are you saying you were seduced?''

"Swept off my feet.'' she told him.

"Now you know how Sara and the other ladies who once owned the Clayborne ring probably felt after they found themselves in bed with the man who was drawn by the ring.''

"An entirely different matter,'' she assured him. "Those three ladies were all hopelessly compromised after the night. Their fates were sealed after they'd been seduced because of the rigid rules of their times.''

Flint chuckled. "And you don't think your fate is just as sealed?''

"Times have changed,'' she retorted.

"Not for you they haven't.''

"What are you talking about?" Rani demanded, a faint trace of wariness filtering into her expression.

Flint realized she was now hovering somewhere on the line between renewed caution and the playful mood that had swept over her in the aftermath of their sensual union. He decided he preferred the playfulness. The last thing he wanted tonight was to alarm her. There would be time enough in the future to impress upon her that she was going to share the same fate as the other women who had owned the ring.

"I was only teasing you," Flint said easily, beginning to trace a curling pattern around the tip of her breast. He smiled to himself as the nipple began to tighten in reaction. She was wonderfully responsive to him. It was as though she'd been made for him. Flint had learned long ago not to question a free gift or a stroke of good fortune. A man grabbed at opportunity when it crossed his path and held on for dear life.

Rani seemed to relax. Her smile returned, warming her eyes with sweet, sensual promise. "What are you doing?"

"Having fun."

"If you're going to play the game, you have to be a full participant."

He looked down at her. "You're still a bossy little thing, aren't you?"

"Still?"

"According to the legend, the ladies all turn sweet and willing after the big seduction."

She smiled. "You keep forgetting that your business is debunking legends, not proving them to be true." She put her arms around his neck. "Come here," she ordered throatily. "I'll show you sweet and willing."

"Yes, ma'am."

Seven

Rani awoke to the sound of the bedroom closet door being opened. For a moment she lay still, trying to assimilate both the memories of the night and the fact that it was morning. Life had changed overnight. She wasn't sure how to deal with the change.

The closet door squeaked, and there was a shuffling sound. Hangers scraped along the wooden rod. Blinking sleepily Rani turned and peered across the room. Zipp was sitting on the foot of the bed, watching intently as Flint hung three work shirts and a couple of pairs of pants beside Rani's brightly colored garments. His clothing looked somber and masculine next to her own.

"What in the world is going on?" Rani sat up, grabbing for the sheet as it fell aside. She had never gotten around to putting on her nightgown last night. Flint was fully dressed in his customary jeans and faded shirt. She felt awkward and shy in her nakedness, overly conscious of her hair falling in a tousled mass onto her shoulders. "What are you doing Flint?" Even as she stared at him he reached down to the battered leather bag at his feet and removed several pairs of socks. These he set about placing in one of the drawers of the dresser.

"I'm just getting comfortable." He arranged the socks in neat, orderly rows and then added a stack of masculine underwear.

"Comfortable! It looks more like you're moving in."

He grinned and shoved the drawer closed. "No sense running back and forth to the other cottage every morning. Of course I'm moving in. What did you expect after last night?" He was beside the bed in two long strides, bending down to kiss her fully on her astonished, upturned mouth.

"But, Flint..." The confused protest was blocked by the kiss. Rani found herself crushed firmly back against the pillows. When Flint released her mouth he looked satisfied. No, it was more than satisfied, Rani decided. There was a distinctly male kind of arrogance about him that morning and it would need watching.

"You," he told her, surveying her critically, "are a very interesting sight in the mornings." He reached down to pat her tousled head. "Nice and warm and rumpled."

"Rumpled!"

"And grumpy. What you need is a morning coffee. I'll go get it started."

"Flint, wait a minute. Where do you think you're going? We have to talk about this."

"Later," he promised from halfway down the hall.

Rani sat staring after him, totally at a loss. It was just as she had predicted the first night she had met him. Give the man an inch and he would grab a mile. One night in her bed and he was moving in on her without even asking permission. It was outrageous. It was also entirely her own fault.

She had to say one thing for herself: when she finally did decide to take risks with a man she had certainly done it in a spectacular manner.

Feeling alarmingly helpless, Rani pushed back the covers and padded quickly into the bathroom. She needed a hot shower before she could deal with Flint Cottrell. She undoubtedly would need a great deal more than a hot shower, but she couldn't imagine what it would be that would do the trick. Cottrell was outside her ken, a man from another world. *And she had let him make love to her last night.* What on earth had she been thinking of to allow that to happen? More importantly, she wasn't sure what to do about the situation now.

It was the way she had awakened to find him calmly moving his things into her bedroom that really brought home the enormity of the situation, she decided as she stood under the hot spray and tried to analyze the mess in which she found herself. If Flint had politely retreated to his own cottage that morning and had made it clear he would only return when and if she wished, Rani thought she might have been able to deal with the traumatic events of the previous night. She would have retained some sense of control, some sense of safety. Instead he had simply assumed that the one-night stand was the beginning of a full-fledged vacation affair.

Rani groaned to herself in the shower. It wasn't that she had wanted a one-night stand, but neither had she intended to start an affair with a man like Flint Cottrell. She was experiencing that trapped feeling again, and she didn't know what to do about it. It was, after all, her own fault that she had found herself in bed with Flint.

She couldn't blame him and she couldn't hate him, she realized. The night before had been uniquely wonderful. She had been a thoroughly willing party in the seduction. Although she was feeling wary and ambivalent now, she knew she couldn't bring herself to regret the previous night's lovemaking.

Rani just wished she didn't feel on the defensive. That much was definitely Flint's fault. He had a lot of nerve to simply move into her bedroom after only a single night in her bed.

Gathering her determination and her willpower around her as though it were an invisible suit of armor, Rani dressed in a pair of fuchsia pants and a fuchsia-striped knit pullover. She put her hair up in its assertive little knot and headed boldly for the kitchen.

Zipp was in his usual position on the windowsill, soaking up the early morning sun. Flint was standing near the stove, eyeing the contents of a frying pan.

"You like your eggs up or over?"

Rani thought about it. "Over."

He nodded. "So do I. This is going to be easy, isn't it?"

"What's going to be easy?" She picked up the mug of coffee that was waiting for her.

"Living together."

Rani coughed as a swallow of very hot coffee went down awkwardly. "Flint, this is going a little too fast for me."

"Don't worry, I'll handle everything."

He spoke with a confident assurance that left Rani with almost nothing to say. She watched, bemused, as he deftly served up the eggs, added toast and brought the two plates over to the table. She wanted to argue or scold. She wanted to regain control of the relationship. She wanted to reassert her ownership of the kitchen if nothing else. But when she met his emerald-green gaze, Rani found herself meekly accepting the plate of eggs and toast.

"Thank you," she mumbled. It was those eyes of his that were her undoing. Perhaps she could have fought the bold way he was acting if it hadn't been for the deep hunger and the barely visible trace of uncertainty that flared briefly in the green depths of his gaze. He was acting as if he had every right in the world to take over her life, but underneath he knew he could do nothing unless she accepted him.

The fact that he was pushing his luck and knew it startled Rani. A part of her found the actions unexpectedly endearing. Another part of her found them incredibly attractive. She didn't know why she should find herself so thoroughly fascinated by a man who came nowhere near her inner image of the right kind of man for her, but Rani was forced to admit the truth. Flint was square in the middle of her small, mountain vacation world, and she could no more bring herself to kick him out than she could have evicted Zipp.

She had taken the sort of risk she had never planned to take. The deed was done, even if it did seem strangely unreal. She might as well commit herself to the excitement and the fantasy because she couldn't possibly terminate the reality.

"How are the eggs?" But Flint was asking another question as he sat down across from Rani, and both of them knew it.

Rani took a delicate bite of toast and egg. "They're very good," she whispered carefully.

"Just right?"

"Yes. Just right."

He grinned again, showing a flash of strong white teeth in an expression that some might have termed feral. Green eyes gleamed in satisfaction. "Good. I'm glad you're pleased."

Rani decided to make some attempt at directing the conversation at least. "What are your plans for the day?"

"The usual. I'll spend the morning on the article, do some work in the garden later on and then we can take the boat ride you mentioned yesterday."

She blinked. "Oh, yes. The rowboat trip. I'd forgotten about it."

"You promised me a picnic," he reminded her.

"Did I?"

"Uh-huh." He glanced down at the flat black metal watch on his wrist. "I'll probably be ready to go around one o'clock. I like tuna fish."

"I'll keep that in mind."

He didn't seem to notice the wry tone of her voice. Instead Flint went blithely on, talking about the weather, the section of the garden he planned to work in for a couple of hours that day and how he would continue to use the small cottage for his writing. By the time breakfast was finished, Rani felt as if she'd been caught up in a huge, gentle wave. There seemed no strong reason to fight it, so she stopped trying. When Flint got up from the table and leaned down to kiss her goodbye in a casually proprietary fashion, she obediently lifted her face for the caress.

"Don't forget the tuna fish sandwiches," he said as he slammed cheerfully through the kitchen door with Zipp trotting after him.

Rani sat for a long, thoughtful moment, staring at the closed door. Then, shaking her head over her own odd mood, she got up to clear the table.

"Are you ready? We'll take the Jeep down to the lake. No more hikes through the woods," Flint said as he came back through the kitchen door at twelve-thirty that afternoon. He had spent the last hour and a half in the garden, Rani knew, but he'd showered and changed his clothes. He glanced around until he spotted the bulging black-and-white-striped tote bag sitting on the table. "Is that lunch?"

She smiled. "That's it. You're in luck. I had some tuna fish."

He nodded, obviously pleased, and picked up the tote bag. "Then let's get going."

"You're awfully eager to start rowing."

"I'm eager to start eating, not rowing," he said. "I can't even remember the last time I went on a picnic." Flint glanced down at Zipp who was eyeing the tote bag with interest. "You're on your own, cat. We'll be back by sundown."

Zipp put on his most wistfully endearing expression, but Flint ignored him, taking Rani's arm instead and striding purposefully toward the front door.

"I thought we could stop at the post office on the way," Rani said, hurrying to keep up with Flint's long, eager stride.

"No problem."

He was in a very amiable frame of mind, Rani decided. It was probably the prospect of free home-cooked food. And possibly the prospect of more free homemade love tonight. Both of which she was providing, Rani reminded herself. She mentally shied away from the long-term ramifications of her decisions.

Mike Slater's nondescript compact was parked outside the Reed Lake Post Office when Flint wheeled the Jeep into a slot near the door. Rani glanced at the familiar vehicle and felt a small pang of anxiety.

"I'll be right back," she said quickly. It would be best if Flint stayed in the Jeep.

"That's okay. I'll come with you." He was already opening the Jeep's door.

Rani glanced again at the artist's car. "Uh, Mike's inside."

Flint lifted one heavy brow in a faint challenge. "So?"

"So I don't want any embarrassing remarks, Flint Cottrell, do I make myself clear?" It was the first time she had been anything resembling assertive all day. Flint eyed her with amused interest.

"I wouldn't think of making any embarrassing remarks. Stop worrying."

Rani shot him a warning glance and turned to push aside the glass door. Flint was right behind her. Both of them nearly collided with Mike who was ambling toward the door from the inside, absently sorting through some mail. He looked up, nodded politely toward Flint and then smiled easily at Rani. There was the faintest of questions in his eyes.

"Hi, Rani. Thought I might have missed you today. Got time for an iced tea over at the café?"

Flint spoke before Rani could answer. "No, she doesn't." He gave Rani a small push in the direction of the counter. "Better hustle, honey. I'm starving."

Rani dug in her heels and summoned up an apologetic smile for Mike. "Sorry, Mike. I really do have to hurry. I'm afraid I've made some plans for the afternoon."

"I see." Mike's mouth lifted with faint, good-natured acceptance of the situation. "Maybe some other time." He didn't look at Flint.

"She's going to be tied up for the rest of her stay here," Flint said coolly.

Mike kept his eyes on Rani's flushed features. "I get the picture."

"I'm sorry, Mike," Rani rushed to say, feeling warm and uncomfortable as she sensed Flint's quietly aggressive challenge. "I'm definitely tied up today, but I'll probably see you tomorrow or the next day when I pick up my mail."

"Get moving, Rani." Flint's voice was soft, but there was a definite hint of laconic command buried in the tone.

Annoyed, she turned her head to meet his gaze. "We're not in that big a hurry, Flint."

"I am."

"I don't know why. We've got the rest of the afternoon ahead of us." But she stalked off toward the counter, common sense telling her it would be best to get Flint out of the post office. He was difficult to manage under the best of circumstances. Faced with what he perceived as a challenge from another man, he might prove downright impossible.

"Hello, Mrs. Hobson," she said brightly. "Anything for me today?"

Mrs. Hobson peered at her over the top of her tiny glasses. The polished stone necklace she wore today matched the bracelet on her wrist. Her blue eyes were alive with interest. Rani knew she hadn't missed the small scene in the lobby. "Not much. A couple of letters is all. How are you doing today, Rani?"

"Just fine, thank you. And yourself, Mrs. Hobson?" Rani took the letters and briskly sorted through them. One was from a co-worker and the other from the neighbor who had volunteered to look after Rani's plants.

"Oh, not bad. John and I are getting ready for a trip to Arizona. Gonna take the motorhome down there and park it for a while in the sunshine. It's gonna get colder and colder in these mountains. Winter's not far off."

"That sounds lovely. More rock hunting?"

"You bet."

Rani grinned suddenly, glancing at the collection of polished stones in the case that sat near the counter. "What do you do with all the rocks you collect, Mrs. Hobson?"

"Keep the good stuff. Use the rest to decorate the front yard," Mrs. Hobson said with an amused shrug. "Nowadays I only bring back the best. When I first got started I brought home everything that took my eye. But you learn. When you've been collecting rocks as long as I have, you learn." But Mrs. Hobson had no intention of being sidetracked from her main interest at the moment. "Friend of yours?" She nodded toward Flint who was lounging against the high post office desk in the lobby. Mike Slater had disappeared.

"A handyman the Andersons hired to do some work around their cottages this winter."

"Funny time of year to do that kind of thing."

Rani wasn't quite sure how to respond to that. It *was* a strange time of year for repairs and gardening. "The Andersons probably wanted the work done now so that they could enjoy the place themselves next spring." It sounded a bit weak, but it was the best Rani could come up with on the spur of the moment.

"Well, he looks as though he ain't afraid of hard work," Mrs. Hobson offered by way of opinion.

"No, Mrs. Hobson. He isn't." Rani was aware of the firmness in her voice and wondered vaguely why she felt obliged to defend Flint. The man could take care of himself.

"Is he staying in the back cottage?"

"Uh, yes."

"What's your artist friend think of all of this?"

"Mrs. Hobson, I . . ."

"You city folks do live exciting lives, don't you?" Mrs. Hobson observed with satisfaction.

"I'll see you tomorrow, Mrs. Hobson."

Flint watched as Rani turned away from the counter and came toward him. She was frowning slightly, wearing that faintly belligerent expression she wore when she was being pushed. He wondered what the woman behind the counter had said to inspire it.

"Ready?" he asked.

"I'm ready. Where's Mike?"

"Gone."

"I can see that," Rani said with careful patience. "What did you say to make him leave so quickly?"

Flint gave her an offended glance. "Hey, he's an artist. Artists are temperamental. Who can figure them?"

"Flint..." she began firmly. Then she floundered to a halt.

Flint smiled. "Let's go get that boat. I can't wait to sink my teeth into that tuna fish sandwich."

She didn't argue. Pleased, and a little relieved, Flint swung the Jeep out of the small parking lot and headed for the tiny marina. There was a small park fronting the lakeshore, and he and Rani walked through it to get to the old wooden building with the dilapidated sign over the doorway that read Gibson's Boats for Rent, by the Day or by the Hour.

"Won't be many more days you can take a boat out and go picnicking on the island," the old man said as he fit the oars in the locks. "You know how to handle these?" he asked Flint.

"I can manage them," Flint said unconcernedly, helping Rani into the small, rocking boat.

"Yup, I guess so." The owner of the boat eyed Flint as he easily unshipped the oars and dipped them into the rippling surface of the lake. "See you in a couple of hours. Five bucks an hour if you go over the two hours you already paid for."

"That's a little steep isn't it?" Flint called back mildly. "Considering the time of the year?" As far as he could see they were the only customers that day.

"Take it or leave it." Gibson didn't appeared worried which choice they made. "Don't reckon you'll stay out more'n a couple of hours, anyhow. It'll start getting a mite chilly on that lake by late afternoon."

Flint didn't argue. He'd discuss the matter with Gibson when he got back. Right now he was more interested in getting on with the picnic. He felt the water's resistance against the oars and leaned into the long pull. Rani sat facing him, her eyes still reflecting the curious combination of uncertainty and acceptance that had been in them when she'd awakened that morning.

Flint searched for the right words, wanting to reassure her and at the same time let her know that everything was settled. He wanted to remove the last of the uncertainty. She was such a cautious, careful creature, he thought. He wanted to impress upon her that the time for wariness was past. All day long he'd been mentally planning what to say to her and how to say it. He gathered himself. "This might be a good time to talk about what happens when your vacation is over, Rani."

He was expecting a tentative response. What he got was an unexpectedly serene smile.

"Why?"

Flint pulled on the oars. "Because I know you'll worry about the future. I don't want you to worry, honey. There's no need."

"I know," she said gently.

A fierce satisfaction mingled with relief washed through him. It was far better than he'd anticipated. She had understood exactly what had happened the night before after all. Flint realized he was probably grinning like a fool, but he couldn't help it. It was going to be much easier than he expected.

"I was afraid you'd fight it," he said softly.

"Were you?"

He inclined his head, combining the action with another long tug on the oars. The boat was skimming swiftly along the surface. Flint glanced back over his shoulder to check the location of the tiny island. "I get the feeling you've been waiting a long time for some guy who fits your mental image of perfection. I wasn't sure how you'd feel when you found yourself in bed with me instead."

"Surprised."

He turned his head to look at her. She was still smiling that serene smile, but now he thought there was a trace of some other expression in the way her mouth curved, something feminine and secretive. "What?"

"Surprised is what I felt when I found myself in bed with you, Flint" she elaborated. "But I think, on the whole, it's going to be an interesting experience. You were perfectly right when you implied I probably hadn't taken enough risks in life. I'm thirty years old, Flint. It's time I took some risks. If I don't, life will pass me by, won't it?"

"Rani, what are you talking about? We're not discussing risks. We're talking about you and me."

She shook her head earnestly, warming to her theme. Belatedly it occurred to Flint that she had done a great deal of thinking on the subject during the day. "I know exactly what we're discussing. Don't worry, Flint, I'm not going to pressure you for a long-term commitment. I'm going to take what you're offering and live life to the fullest for the next three weeks. I've never done this sort of thing before, you know. I've never just jumped into the stream and let the river take me wherever it would."

"Rani..."

"When I woke up this morning, I was feeling confused," she went on candidly. "I was a little scared, I think. There you were, acting as though everything were settled for the next three weeks. Maybe I was a bit resentful at the way you just moved in on me. But I've had plenty of time to think about things and I've decided you were right. It's time I took a risk. I've spent years trying to protect myself, always trying to analyze the extent of a man's commitment before I gave anything of myself."

"Rani, that's what I'm trying to explain to you," Flint broke in, not liking the direction of the conversation. "You don't have to worry about that this time."

"I know. This time I'm just going to enjoy myself. I'm not going to even think about what happens when the vacation is over. I'm going to live for the moment." Her eyes brimmed with a new excitement. "I've probably missed a great deal all these years, Flint. No doubt I've passed up some wonderful experiences because I didn't see any future with the man who was offering those opportunities."

Now he was getting annoyed. "You haven't missed a damn thing, Rani. You were right to be careful."

She shook her head. "No, I overdid it. What's life without a few risks? That's how we grow and change, isn't it, Flint? Risks are what makes life exciting. Oh, I realize this is probably a cliché for you, but for me it's a whole new way of thinking. I feel free. I won't think beyond tomorrow for the next few weeks. Don't worry, Flint. I'm not going to be moody or temperamental. No scenes, I promise. I'm just going to enjoy myself."

"The hell you are," he bit out. "Now listen to me, Rani Garroway. What happened last night was important. It changes a lot of things for us and it changes them permanently, not just for the next three weeks. Do you hear me, lady?"

She nodded, reaching down to fish around inside the black-and-white tote bag. "I hear you, but you can stop worrying, Flint. I feel quite capable of dealing with the situation. You don't have to pretend there's a long-term future involved here. In fact, I'd just as soon you didn't try. I'd rather keep everything strictly honest if you don't mind. I promise not to try to maneuver you into an extended affair or, heaven forbid, marriage, but in exchange I'd like you to promise you won't lie to me because you think that's a way of keeping me cooperative for the next few weeks. Let's agree to be honest with each other, Flint. We're adults. We can take our risks honestly."

"Now just a damn minute," he began savagely, pulling so hard on the oars that the small craft almost leaped out of the water. "You're twisting everything around. I'm trying to talk about a future and you're acting as if you're only in this for the next couple of weeks."

"We both know we're only in this for the next couple of weeks. Why pretend otherwise? Want a potato chip? They're the extra thick kind. They make them with the skins on, but I'm not sure how much real nutrition that adds. I mean, after you've deepfried a slice of potato and poured salt all over it, how much good is left in the poor thing? But it does taste wonderful." She munched cheerfully as she spoke, reaching out to put a chip between his lips.

"Rani, I'm trying to deal seriously with this." Flint ignored the potato chip she was holding quite close to his mouth. "I don't understand you today. What the hell has gotten into you?" And then, quite suddenly, he did understand her. She was scared. She didn't want to talk about the future because she was afraid of it. Rani was hiding the fear behind a veil of feminine bravado. He understood completely, and he could hardly blame her. Giving her a lecture on how he intended to stick around wasn't going to reassure her. It would be best if he just backed off and let her adjust in her own way. Sooner or later she would begin to grow more certain of him. Then they could talk.

"Don't you want the potato chip?" she asked politely.

Flint opened his mouth and crunched the chip very forcefully between his teeth. "Are we going to eat the whole picnic lunch before we get to the island?" he asked softly.

"Nope. Just a few appetizers." She watched him, the anxiety almost hidden beneath the determined brightness of her smile. "Want another chip?"

"Sounds terrific."

The phone rang two evenings later, just as Rani was finishing the task of rinsing the last of the dinner dishes she and Flint had been washing. The past two days had been composed of homey scenes like the present one, interspersed with hours of such compelling passion that Rani had begun to wonder if her life were indeed real. She had never thought real life could contain such a spectrum of quiet happiness and intense excitement. As long as she didn't think about the future, she was free to enjoy it to the hilt.

"I'll get it." Rani tossed a cotton dish towel at Flint. "Here, you can start drying."

He took the cloth with a nod, and Rani headed quickly toward the phone in the living room. Flint had been quite agreeable for the past couple of days, ever since she had squelched his attempt to discuss the future. Perhaps he was secretly relieved at not having to pretend their relationship was of the long-term variety. The last thing she wanted from Flint Cottrell was lies, Rani thought as she lifted the receiver. She could handle anything except lies from him.

"Hello?"

"Miss Garroway, this is Charles Dewhurst. Have I caught you at a bad time?"

Startled, Rani hastily denied any problem. "Not at all, Mr. Dewhurst, but I wasn't expecting to hear from you. Has something happened?'' The ring on her hand briefly caught the lamplight. She looked down at it, frowning.

"Not exactly," Charles Dewhurst said in an apologetic tone. "It's nothing really, just some trade gossip that has reached my ears. I thought I would pass it along, although I hesitate to alarm you."

"Alarm me about what?"

Dewhurst cleared his throat, obviously a bit uncertain about how to proceed. "Well, it's about your Uncle Ambrose, my dear. About the accident back East."

Rani's fingers tightened fractionally on the receiver. "What about the accident?"

"My dear, you must realize that one hears a lot of gossip after a man with your uncle's, uh, reputation, dies. The world of gemstones tends to thrive on mystery and rumor. Your uncle knew a great many people both here and abroad, and more than a few suspected he indulged his talents in, shall we say, somewhat shady ways."

"Please, Mr. Dewhurst. Tell me what the problem is."

She could hear Dewhurst taking a deep breath before continuing. "There is talk, my dear, that your uncle's death was not precisely an accident."

Rani went cold. She also went very still. "Not an accident?"

"Now, I've gone and alarmed you and I had no right to do that. I just felt you should know what sort of things are being said. It's all over now, my dear, and I'm sure there's no reason to be concerned, but when I heard the rumors I thought it my duty to pass them along. Please don't take them too seriously. I only mention them in the first place because you were the one who inherited the jewelry."

"But the jewelry is paste! Mr. Dewhurst, are you suggesting Uncle Ambrose was killed?"

"There is a rumor in the business to that effect, I'm afraid," Dewhurst said with a small sigh.

"But it makes no sense. If the jewelry I inherited is all fake..."

"It seems, Miss Garroway, that some people believe your uncle actually had the Clayborne ring in his possession at the time he died. They think he had not yet made the duplicate of the stone."

Rani caught her breath. "Someone believes the emerald is real? That my uncle might have been killed because of it?"

"That's what I have heard. Please, Miss Garroway, there is no need to get upset. You and I both know that if Ambrose ever did have the ring the original is long gone now."

"But what if someone believes I have it? What if whoever killed Uncle Ambrose doesn't know my uncle had time to make the imitation ring and get rid of the original?"

Dewhurst hastened to reassure her, obviously upset at having caused Rani to worry. "Please, Miss Garroway, don't be unduly alarmed. I have done what I could to squelch the rumor of the stone being real. I have a certain degree of respect in this field and I have let it be known that I personally saw the ring after you inherited it. I have also let it be known that the duplicate is one of Ambrose's finest works, but that it is definitely glass. With any luck my evaluation will become known to the person who may or may not have been responsible for your uncle's death. I'm sure there is little cause for concern. But since you are now officially the ring's owner, I thought it best that you be notified."

"Do your trade rumors indicate who might have been responsible for my uncle's accident, Mr. Dewhurst?" Rani was surprised by the steadiness of her own voice.

"No. There is only some speculative talk about a man who has been on the trail of the ring for years. Someone your uncle apparently dealt with at one time. I'm afraid I know nothing more about him. Please try not to worry, Miss Garroway. Perhaps I shouldn't have called.''

"No," she interrupted quietly, "I'm glad you called. I appreciate your warning.''

"I will do what I can to make certain everyone who might be interested in this affair is aware that I have ascertained the ring is a fake. If there is someone out looking for the ring, he is sure to hear of my assessment. That's probably the best defense under the circumstances. Surely no one would spend time and money continuing to pursue green glass.''

"Thank you, Mr. Dewhurst.''

"You will take care, my dear?''

"Oh, yes," Rani whispered. "I'll take care.'' She hung up the phone, not moving. Blindly, she continued to stare down into the green depths of the ring.

Rani didn't know quite when she realized she wasn't alone in the living room. She only knew that, when she turned slowly to find Flint watching her from the doorway, she experienced no real sense of surprise. She also knew from the look in his eyes that he had overheard her conversation with Dewhurst.

"Mr. Dewhurst says there is a possibility that someone killed my uncle because of this ring." She felt as if she were speaking in a dream. There was a sense of unreality pervading the room. She was trapped.

Flint slowly dried his hands on the towel he was holding. "He's right.''

Eight

It was Zipp who broke the stillness. He ambled in from the kitchen and meowed loudly. Rani reached down to pick him up, holding him protectively. Then her eyes went back to Flint's face. She didn't say a word. Flint swore softly.

"I didn't want you to find out this way," he said.

"I imagine you didn't." Her voice was even but very remote. "Who are you?"

His gaze narrowed as he realized what she was thinking. "I'm not the man who killed your uncle." But he twisted the dish towel savagely, and the small violence drew Rani's attention. She stared at his hand as if he were holding a gun. "Did you hear me, Rani? I'm not the one who killed Ambrose."

"Then who are you?"

"I've told you the truth. I was a friend of your uncle's. I helped him trace the history of the ring."

"And now you want it for yourself." She looked down at her hand. The ring was partially hidden by Zipp's fur. "I don't understand any of this. It's just junk."

"Someone thinks it's real."

"The same someone who killed Uncle Ambrose."

"Rani, for God's sake, stop talking as if you were waiting for me to pull a gun on you."

"Where is your gun, Flint? It was certainly very convenient the other day in the woods when you scared off that stupid hunter." Clutching Zipp so tightly that he squawked mildly in protest, Rani edged back a couple of steps. There was an outside chance she could make it through the door before Flint caught her. He wasn't armed at the moment. She might be able to disappear into the woods before he could get his ugly handgun. It wasn't much of a chance, but in that moment she couldn't think of anything else.

"Please don't run away from me, Rani." His voice was low and harsh.

"You can have the ring," she said, struggling to remove it from her finger without letting go of the cat. "I can't imagine why anyone would want it. Believe me, I don't. Not after all this. Take it, Flint. You've worked hard enough to get it."

"The ring is yours."

It came free of her hand, and she tossed it toward him. Flint made no move to catch it, and it clattered to the floor. "Take it," Rani commanded softly. "Take it and get out."

"I don't want the damned ring. Are you going to sit down and listen while I explain this mess, or are you going to make some idiotic dash into the woods? Make up your mind, Rani. If you're going to run, go ahead and try it. Let's get that part over so we can start talking."

He was reading her mind, Rani decided. Flint knew exactly what she was thinking. But then perhaps he'd seen more than one person in this situation. She was shivering, she realized. Faint ripples of fear and anger flowed through her. She had to control both the fear and the anger or she wouldn't stand a chance. Zipp meowed again.

"You must think me a complete fool," she whispered. "I made it all so easy for you, didn't I? I gave you shelter, fed you and, to top it all off, let you into my bed."

He took a step forward but stopped when she instinctively retreated. Flint's expression hardened. "Do you really think I'd hurt you, Rani?"

She stared at him. She was feeling so disoriented that she couldn't seem to think properly. "You're here because of the ring."

"I'm here because your uncle was killed. He owned that ring and now you own it. I don't want the same thing happening to you that happened to Ambrose. Listen to me, Rani. I'm here to protect you, not hurt you."

"I don't understand."

"I know you don't. Stop figuring out how you're going to make it through the door and start listening to what I'm saying. I did not kill Ambrose. I had nothing to do with his death. But when I heard about the circumstances of his so-called accident, I realized it might have been an act of murder. And if he had been killed, I had to assume it was because of the ring."

"Why should you assume that?"

Flint slung the dish towel over the back of a nearby chair. "Because I knew the ring wasn't fake."

Rani caught her breath. "What are you talking about."

His mouth twisted wryly. "Oh, the stone you've got there could easily be paste. Most likely is, judging from what your uncle's jeweler friend has told you. I'm no authority on gems. But when Ambrose first came into possession of the ring, he told me it was the real thing. He also told me that he intended to keep it, not copy it. He said it was going to be the one perfect stone in his collection. It was too beautiful, too valuable and contained too much history to be cut up and sold on the black market. The Clayborne ring was the one genuine piece in his collection. Don't you see, Rani? If I knew the emerald was for real, so did any number of other people. Ambrose sent me a letter shortly before his death telling me he was worried. Someone else was on the trail of the ring, and he planned to take precautions. He didn't spell out the precautions. I didn't get the letter for several weeks because I was in North Africa. By the time I picked up my mail your uncle was dead."

"So you immediately came looking for the ring?" Rani challenged.

"I learned that whoever had arranged your uncle's accident hadn't gotten his hands on the ring. Your uncle's collection of fakes was being held by his lawyer, and according to the itemized list, a ring matching the description of the Clayborne ring was still with the rest of the stuff Ambrose had created when he died. The police went under the assumption the accident was for real. They didn't suspect murder. I might not have either if I hadn't had your uncle's letter and if I hadn't known that one item in Ambrose's collection wasn't a fake. I decided that if Ambrose had been killed whoever had done it might still be following the ring. I went looking for the person who had inherited Ambrose's collection of fakes."

"I see. What exactly did you intend to do when you found me?"

"Keep an eye on you for a while. I wasn't sure if anyone would make another try for the ring, but I wanted to be around if it happened. I felt I owed it to Ambrose."

She closed her eyes in brief anguish. "I certainly made it easy for you to keep an eye on the ring, didn't I? Why didn't you tell me all this when you arrived on my doorstep?"

"Because I wasn't even sure if Ambrose had been killed. I only suspected it. I didn't know at first where you fitted in. You seemed to be an innocent bystander in all this. I didn't want to alarm you. I just wanted to keep tabs on you until I knew for sure what was going on. I didn't even know if the stone in the ring was still the genuine emerald. Ambrose had said he was going to take precautions. He might have made a duplicate before he died and hidden the real emerald. Making copies was his profession. It would have been natural for him to attempt to protect the ring by creating a fake."

"Since this is a fake, where's the real one?"

Flint ran a hand through his hair. "I don't know. There's no telling where Ambrose might have stashed it. My concern was that whoever was after it wouldn't know he was following a piece of glass. He still might be willing to kill to get hold of the ring."

Rani shook her head in mute denial. "Why should you have felt obliged to protect me? You didn't know me. Why go through all this trouble just to keep an eye on whoever inherited the ring?"

"I told you, Rani, your uncle was my friend."

"The way you move around, you've probably got a lot of acquaintances. Do you feel this sort of obligation toward all of them?"

His mouth thinned at her skeptical tone. "I said Ambrose was a friend. I may know a lot of people, Rani, but I don't have a lot of friends. Ambrose was one."

"So you looked me up out of some noble sense of friendship?"

"Damn it, Rani, it *was* a sense of friendship that brought me here. If you want to know the truth, it was more than that. Maybe if I'd had that letter from Ambrose earlier, I could have kept him from getting killed."

"It was guilt that brought you here then?" She knew she was pushing him, but she couldn't help it. She felt hurt and angry and still somewhat afraid.

"I only knew I had to check up on whoever had inherited the ring. When I traced it to you I wasn't sure how to handle things. I thought it would be easier just to hang around for a while and see what developed. I told you I didn't want to scare you unless it was absolutely necessary. Like Dewhurst, I was hoping that word would spread the ring had been duplicated and the stone in this one was fake. That information should have kept you from being interesting to whoever had killed Ambrose."

"All that talk of tracking down the ring because you were writing an article on it was just a convenient lie? You must have lied to the Andersons, too, to convince them to give you the job. Were all those lies and fabrications simpler than telling me the truth?"

"I've never lied to you. I am writing an article on that ring. I would have wanted to know what became of it even if I hadn't been concerned that someone might be after it. I never lied to the Andersons, either. I asked for a job and I'm doing the work."

Zipp wriggled in Rani's grasp, demanding to be released. She hesitated because there was a vague element of comfort to be found in clutching him in front of her like a shield. But when he growled to show he was serious she slowly lowered him to the floor. Zipp trotted over to Flint, stroked his tail once or twice against Flint's jeans and then headed back toward the kitchen. The cat was clearly unconcerned about the small drama taking place in the living room. Rani watched him disappear, her mind whirling with confusion and hurt.

"I'll admit you're a hard worker, Flint," she said at last. "The Andersons, at least, are getting their money's worth. All in all this probably rates as one of your better gardening jobs, doesn't it? Or is sleeping with the lady of the house a common fringe benefit in your line of work?"

Flint's eyes were shuttered and cold as he moved forward to catch hold of Rani. She sensed his intention, but she didn't have time to evade his grasp. His big hands closed around her upper arms as he forced her to look at him. "I'm sleeping with you because I want you and you want me. It's as simple as that. Don't drag our personal relationship into this."

She glared at him in open amazement. "Don't drag our personal relationship into this!" she repeated. "Are you joking? That's what this whole mess is all about, isn't it? You made what might have been a business relationship or a matter of obligation into a very personal relationship. Or don't you see it that way? I realize that you probably view our . . . our affair as a casual and convenient little romp but that doesn't mean I, at least, don't find it a very personal matter."

"Don't get hysterical on me, Rani."

"I am not hysterical, I'm mad!"

"You're hardly a woman scorned. Don't act like one."

She tried to free herself. When he wouldn't release her, she glanced pointedly down at his hands. He followed her look and reluctantly released her arms. When he dropped his hands to his sides, she stepped away, folding her arms across her breasts. She came to a halt in front of the window, staring unseeingly out into the garden at the front of the house.

"You should have told me the truth, Flint. Right from the start. It wasn't fair of you to let me think you were here only to write the article and pick up a few bucks doing repairs for the Andersons. I feel used."

"You have no right to feel used," he told her harshly. "I haven't used you and you know it. Maybe I should have told you the truth, but I've already explained I wasn't sure what was going on. I didn't want to alarm you. I just wanted to keep an eye on you and the ring for a while. If I'd walked in here that first night and told you there was a possibility someone might kill you for the ring, how would you have reacted?"

"We'll never know, will we? You didn't handle it that way."

"I'll tell you how you would have reacted. You'd have thought I was insane. You'd have been scared to death and you wouldn't have let me in the front door."

"The only difference now is that you're in the front door."

He came up behind her. "Rani, I didn't realize your friend Dewhurst would hear about the rumors surrounding Ambrose's death. I didn't know he'd call and warn you. Hell, I was hoping your uncle's death really was an accident. With any luck this whole thing would have blown over in a few months."

"And having done your duty, you could slip back out of my life the same way you slipped into it," she concluded bitterly.

"Stop it, Rani."

"What made you think you were qualified to protect me if I was in danger? You're a handyman, a gardener, someone who writes articles for treasure hunting magazines."

"I told you, I've done some work as a bodyguard," he said stiffly. "Some security work."

"Oh, that's right. I'd forgotten your varied résumé. Do all bodyguards get to sleep with their female clients?"

Flint jerked her around to face him again. "That's what's really bothering you, isn't it?" he charged. "You're madder than hell because I had the nerve to take you to bed, not because I didn't tell you the whole truth. You've decided I took advantage of you."

"Well, didn't you?"

"Lady, we would have ended up in bed regardless of what story I'd told you the night I arrived."

"Not necessarily!"

"Want to bet?" He pulled her closer.

Rani's unstable mixture of emotions exploded. "No, I do not want to bet. Nor do I want you trying to prove how irresistible you are. What I want is for you to get out of here, Flint Cottrell. You say you're here to guard me, so, okay, start guarding. Go fetch that big, ugly gun of yours and start patrolling the perimeter or whatever it is guards are supposed to do. Go on, get out of my cottage. You can spend the night walking around outside watching for jewel thieves."

"I'm going to spend the night in your bed, damn it!"

"Not a chance."

Something that might have been desperation moved across his face. "Rani, honey, listen to me. I know you're angry, but the bottom line in all this is that nothing between us has changed. We're involved. You can't kick me out."

"Want to bet?" Deliberately she mimicked his own earlier challenge. "I'm ordering you out of this cottage, Flint."

"No." He shook his head firmly. "You can't."

She took a deep breath. "You won't leave willingly?"

"I'm not leaving. Period."

"In that case, I don't have much choice, do I?"

His gaze softened. "You don't want a choice, Rani. You want me to stay and you know it. Stop fighting both of us."

She ducked out from under his arm, striding down the hall to the bedroom. "You're bigger than I am, Flint. If you won't go on request, I can't force you."

"What the hell are you up to now?" he demanded, following her down the hall.

"If you won't leave, I'll have to do the leaving. I am not spending another night in this cottage with you." She opened the closet door, shoved aside his clothes and dragged out her suitcase. Tossing it on the bed, she began filling it with the contents of her side of the closet.

"Rani, cut it out. You're acting like a child."

"I thought you said I was acting like a woman scorned."

"You're being ridiculous."

She shrugged and reached for a stack of underwear. He put his hand out and shoved the drawer closed.

"All right, all right. If you're going to be this way about it, I'll leave," Flint said through gritted teeth.

She stood very still, waiting. "Goodbye, Flint."

"You're going to regret this, you know. You're hurting both of us."

"I, for one, will be far more hurt if I allow you to spend another night in my bed."

"Honey, that's just not true. When you've calmed down, you'll realize it."

"Get out of here, Flint."

He stood looking down at her for another moment. She saw the frustration and the leashed anger in him and wondered if it would escape. But in the end Flint controlled himself as she had somehow known he would. Without a word he turned and walked out of the room.

Rani stood where she was until she heard the kitchen door slam shut. Then she sank slowly down onto the bed and huddled into herself. She concentrated her full attention on trying to keep the tears from escaping between her lashes.

Two hours later Flint gave up trying to sleep and swung his legs over the edge of the decrepit old bed he was using in the back cottage. He was still wearing his jeans. He hadn't bothered to undress completely because a part of him refused to admit he was really going to spend the whole night in his small cottage. For the fourth or fifth time he paced silently over to the window and stared out into the night. Rani's bedroom light had finally been switched off. It had been on a long time after he'd left.

She was lying there in the darkness, but he doubted if she was asleep any more than he was. She would be thinking of all that had been said that evening. What he really wanted her to think about was what had not been said. Had she realized the full import of that yet? When and if she did, would it make any difference to her? He had no way of knowing how she would respond even if she did admit the truth to herself.

Restlessly Flint turned away from the window and walked over to the refrigerator. It was humming noisily in the kitchen alcove. Absently he gave it a kick to quiet it and then he opened it to see if there was anything interesting inside. It was empty except for the last of the six-pack. He reached for the beer and popped the top. Can in one hand, he went back to his post at the window.

She couldn't be asleep. She must be lying there thinking about what she had learned that evening.

Flint felt a distinct sense of irritation toward Charles Dewhurst. If he hadn't called with his belated warning, the present situation wouldn't have arisen. Flint could have told Rani the truth in his own time and in his own way.

She didn't understand why he hadn't been completely honest with her right from the start. Flint had to admit she had a point. His main goal had been to protect her without alarming her, but she didn't seem to appreciate that. Perhaps he should have just told her the truth. It would have scared the hell out of her, though, and possibly with no real justification.

There had been no proof that anyone had deliberately killed Ambrose. Flint was surprised the rumors of murder were strong enough to reach all the way to Dewhurst. Even the police hadn't been concerned about the possibility that the accident was anything more than what it seemed. Still, the fact remained that Dewhurst had heard it somewhere and had called Rani to warn her.

The whole thing had disintegrated into an idiotic mess because he'd mishandled everything that first night. Flint groaned and took a swallow of beer. He should have told her the facts right at the beginning.

But if he had done that she would never have felt comfortable or relaxed around him. At best she might have treated him like a professional bodyguard. She would have tried to keep the relationship on a businesslike basis. At worst she would have fled back to her safe, secure world, leaving him to chase after her and try to convince her to let him into her life. As a handyman-gardener who was trying to write an article on the side, Flint knew he was a lot less threatening to her than if he'd walked in the front door and told her he was there to protect her from her uncle's murderer.

Perhaps he'd taken the selfish route, but in retrospect Flint was inclined to think that, given the same situation, he would have done things the same way. He had known the moment she'd opened the door to him during the storm that

Rani wasn't going to be just another job. He had known she was going to change his whole life.

When a man found a woman capable of changing his entire life, he probably didn't think as clearly as he would under normal circumstances. Maybe he'd behaved like an ass.

The real question tonight was whether Rani had settled down and really thought about the evening's events. Flint stood silently at the window, drinking the beer and reflecting on his own stupidity.

Rani was wide awake, lying quietly in bed and staring at the play of shadows on the ceiling when she became aware of the familiar figure of a man standing in the garden outside her window. Zipp jumped lightly off the bed and bounded up onto the windowsill. Ducking inside the sheer curtains, he pressed his nose to the glass and meowed inquiringly.

On the other side of the window, Flint didn't move for a moment. Then he put out his hands and calmly opened the window. Rani watched with a curious fascination as the window was raised. The Andersons really should hire a handyman to fix the broken lock, she thought.

"Hello, Zipp." Flint made no move to enter the room. He leaned inside the open window, letting chilled air into the room as he casually scratched the cat's ears. Zipp purred loudly for a moment and then something caught his attention. He dived through the window and disappeared. Flint continued to lean into the room, his elbows resting on the sill. "You awake?" he asked quietly.

"I'm awake."

There was a silence for another moment and then he said carefully, "I've been thinking."

"So have I."

"About the same things, I wonder?"

"I have no idea," she murmured. Rani felt as if she were back in the dreamlike atmosphere that had enveloped her earlier in the evening. Nothing seemed quite real except for Flint's inescapable presence.

"You're not going to make this easy for me, are you, Rani?"

"What do you want me to do?"

He exhaled slowly. "I'm afraid to ask. That may not seem strange to you, but it is to me. I can't remember the last time I was afraid to ask for something that was important."

He probably couldn't remember the last time he'd ever actually asked for something politely in the first place, Rani decided with a detached sort of amusement. Like Zipp, Flint was far more accustomed to simply taking what he wanted. "Why are you afraid this time?"

In the moonlight his bare shoulders lifted in a self-deprecatory shrug. "Because I'm nervous about the answer, I guess. Most things aren't this important."

Rani didn't know what to say to that. She sensed the honesty of his words, but she wasn't sure what to do next. All her life she had been careful. Only this man had the ability to make her reckless. From her point of view that represented a truly awesome power. The safest course of action was to keep him at a distance. But Rani wasn't even sure she had that option any longer. She had been doing a great deal of thinking during the past couple of hours and some conclusions were unavoidable. "Am I really that important to you, Flint?" she heard herself ask gently.

He looked at her through the shadows. "If you weren't important, I probably wouldn't have screwed things up this badly. Rani, I need to know if you've thought about what else happened earlier."

"I've thought of little else."

Flint hesitated. "Did you realize exactly what happened tonight after the phone call?"

It was her turn to hesitate. "I realized I didn't react the way I should have reacted under the circumstances," she finally admitted.

He nodded. "You were madder than hell and a little confused, but you didn't really believe I was the murderer."

"It did cross my mind initially," she managed to point out dryly. He wasn't going to have it all his own way.

Flint came through the window, slipping into the darkened room like a cat returning from an evening's hunt. "It may have crossed your mind, but you weren't worried about that aspect for very long, were you? Why not, Rani? It was the logical assumption. Dewhurst had just told you that someone was after the ring. You know nothing about me except what I've told you." Flint moved over to the bed and stood looking down at her. "So why didn't you call the cops the second I left?"

"Maybe it was nothing more than female pride that kept me from doing it," she retorted.

"Pride?" That took him back. It wasn't the answer he'd been expecting.

"I might not have wanted to admit to myself or the sheriff that I'd been having an affair with a murderer."

Flint sat down on the edge of the bed, his weight making a heavy impression on the mattress. He rested his elbows on his knees, his hands clasped loosely in front of him. "You really aren't going to make this easy for me, are you?"

"What do you want me to say, Flint? That I've been lying here realizing I couldn't suspect you as a murderer because of the way you make love to me? That I'm far too involved with you to let myself believe you're a danger to me? That all my feminine instincts tell me I can trust you? That deep down I believe you intended no harm, that you only wanted to protect me? Is that the sort of thing you want to hear me say?''

He inclined his head but didn't turn to look at her. "Something like that.''

"Ah," she said knowingly. "Perhaps that wasn't quite as much as you wanted. Maybe you wanted to hear a little more.''

"Such as?''

"Such as I'm probably falling in love with you and that's the real reason I couldn't possibly believe you're a danger to me?'' Her voice was a soft whisper of sound in the darkness. She wasn't sure he heard until he moved.

"Rani.'' Her name was a deep sigh of masculine relief. He came down beside her on the bed, gathering her into his arms and holding her fiercely against his bare chest. He buried his face in her hair. "Oh, God, Rani.''

"You're cold," she heard herself say, touching him with a sense of wonder. "What on earth were you doing running around outside without a jacket?''

"I was hoping you'd let me warm up in your bed," he said into her hair. He stroked her with his big, callused hand. "Are you falling in love with me, sweetheart?''

"Does it matter?''

"It matters. I want you to love me, Rani. I want it very much. I swear I'll take care of you.''

"You keep saying that.''

"I mean it.''

Rani sighed, relaxing against him. "I know.''

"You trust me?''

"I don't seem to have much choice," she admitted.

"Maybe neither one of us has a choice.'' His mouth closed over hers with a heavy, dark need. The deep kiss was both an act of claiming and an act of gratitude.

She should be more afraid of the power he had over her, Rani told herself as her lips parted beneath the pressure of his. But there was no way she could ever really fear this man, and she knew it now. It was the unavoidable, inescapable conclusion she had reached as she had laid alone in the darkness thinking about the evening's events.

She knew with a sure, womanly instinct that Flint Cottrell was the man fate had chosen to teach her about the reckless, uninhibited power of passion and love.

Nine

The sun was forging an unsteady path between a coalescing mass of gray clouds when Rani stirred into wakefulness the next morning. She knew Flint was already wide awake beside her, although he hadn't disturbed her by moving. He was like Zipp in a lot of ways, she thought in sleepy amusement. There was a lazy alertness about him that seemed to be part of his basic makeup even when he was sound asleep.

She turned in his arms, and Flint stretched luxuriously. "What I'd really like to know," he announced, leaning over to kiss her, "is what rumors Dewhurst actually heard."

"That's not the first thing you're supposed to say in the morning."

Flint propped himself on his elbow and rested one hand possessively on her breast. He tilted a lazy brow. "No? What am I supposed to say?"

You're supposed to say I love you, Rani thought silently. Aloud she murmured, "Something along the lines of how cute and cuddly I look in the morning, I believe."

He gave her a slow grin. "How cute and cuddly you look in the morning!" he exclaimed dutifully. "Also sexy as hell." He moved his thumb on the tip of her breast and watched with interest as the nipple reacted. Satisfied with the firming peak, he slid one foot down the calf of her leg. Then he deliberately pushed his knee between hers, his eyes never leaving her face. His hand made its way over her breast, trailing slowly toward the soft nest of hair below her flat stomach. "Very cute. Very cuddly."

"So are you. She wound her arm around his neck and pulled his head back down to hers. Flint obeyed the summons willingly, his mouth closing over hers as his fingers snagged gently in the nest he had found.

She loved the feel of his big, callused hands, Rani thought as Flint bore her back against the pillows. Such strong, careful, gentle hands. Hands that could coax a garden into shape. It was hard to remember that once she had seen a gun in those hands. He was meant to grow things, not kill things.

"You should stick to gardening," she told him in a soft whisper.

"You think I'm good at it?" He touched her intimately until she sighed and lifted herself against his hand.

"You're very good at it. Oh, *Flint!*"

Zipp roused himself in disgust, jumped down off the bed and stalked off to the kitchen to find his morning spot on the windowsill. Humans had a way of getting their priorities mixed up. This was the time of day for breakfast and a nap in the sunlight.

It was a long while before Rani and Flint joined the cat in the kitchen. When Rani finally did start breakfast for the three of them, she was feeling healthy, vibrant and very much alive. Her hair was in its usual knot, and she wore a brilliant coral shirt with her jeans. The ring on her hand glinted in the morning light as she flipped pancakes.

Sitting at the kitchen table, a cup of coffee in one hand, Flint watched her with a hunger that wasn't just for the pancakes. Rani could feel his eyes on her as she worked, and the sensation was a little disquieting. It was difficult to tell sometimes exactly what Flint Cottrell was thinking. He'd spent too many years learning to conceal his emotions.

"What was it you started to say about Mr. Dewhurst this morning?" she asked, deciding to get Flint talking.

There was a slight pause behind her. "I was just wondering how Dewhurst heard the rumors about Ambrose's death. Did he say who had told him?"

Rani shook her head. "Only that there was some gossip in the trade."

"Dewhurst is a long way from the East Coast where your uncle was killed."

"True, but he was a longtime business associate of my uncle's. If there was talk about a murder, it makes sense it might have gotten back to him. He said something about a man who had been on the trail of the Clayborne ring for many years."

Flint was thoughtful. "A lot of people have wanted that ring over the years. So far as I know, none of them has wanted it badly enough to kill for it."

Rani glanced down at the gem. "How valuable is it, Flint. If this was the real thing, what do you think it would be worth?"

"Hard to say what it's value would be to a collector, but Ambrose once told me that if the stone were removed, cut up and sold a man might get somewhere in the neighborhood of a hundred grand if he knew what he was doing.

Cutting up the stone would devalue it. No telling what it's worth whole.''

Rani swallowed. "That's a nice neighborhood."

"Whoever cut and sold the real stone would have to know what he was doing and who he was dealing with, Rani. Not everyone has access to that kind of skill."

"My uncle would have known what to do and who to contact." Rani sighed.

"True. But Ambrose told me this was the one piece of jewelry he wasn't going to duplicate. He wanted to keep the Clayborne ring. He was fascinated by the history surrounding it. It wasn't just another pretty trinket to him."

Rani piled the pancakes on two plates and carried them over to the table. "But he still might have copied it just to protect the original."

"That's a possibility," Flint agreed, accepting his plate with the enthusiasm he reserved for Rani's cooking.

There was no doubt that he liked having her cook for him, Rani thought with concealed humor. She was a decent cook but not a great one. She doubted it was her culinary skill that appealed so much to him. It was more subtle, more primitive than that. Rani sensed it had to do with the symbolic fact that she was doing the cooking for him. He liked eating her food because in a nonverbal way it established a very distinct, very basic bond between them. Until now Rani hadn't realized just how basic cooking for a man could be.

"Assuming that he did decide to duplicate the ring, where would he have hidden the original?" she asked, buttering her pancakes.

"I don't know." Flint munched reflectively. "A safe-deposit box that we don't know about perhaps. Somewhere in his shop. The possibilities are endless."

"But he would have wanted someone to find the ring eventually," Rani pointed out. "He wouldn't have hidden it so that no one would ever find it."

"He may not have had time to set up the hiding place and the clues." Flint forked up another bite. "We don't even know for sure he was killed because of the ring. I told you, Rani, it's just a suspicion."

"One that Dewhurst shares, apparently."

"Yeah. I'd sure like to know how he heard that particular suspicion. Maybe he knows someone who could shed some light on this mess for us."

Rani put down her fork. "What do we do now, Flint?"

"The same thing I've been doing all along. Exercise due caution for a while. If nothing happens we can assume eventually that either no one really is after the ring or that whoever is after it has heard it's a fake and is looking elsewhere."

"How long do we exercise this 'due caution'?"

"Until things feel right," Flint said casually.

Rani stared at him in astonishment. "Until they feel right? What on earth does that mean?"

"It means I'm operating on a gut feeling that I can't really justify with evidence."

She frowned. "A feeling that something is wrong?"

He nodded. "Don't worry. I've been off base before when I've had this feeling. I could be wrong this time, too."

He looked up, his gaze locking with hers. "It's all I've got to go on, Rani."

Rani couldn't think of anything to say to that.

The pattern of the day fell into its normal routine, although Rani didn't see how that was possible. Surely, after the realization she had made the previous night that she was falling in love with Flint, something significant should have changed in the environment. But everything went on as it had for the past several days. Flint seemed to have accepted with magnificent calm what to her was a momentous discovery. It was rather irritating.

It was late in the afternoon when Rani decided to run into town to check the post office and pick up some items for dinner. She wandered out into the garden to find Flint. He was coiling a hose near a stack of gardening tools when she found him.

"Give me a minute to change my shirt and I'll come with you," he said.

Rani nodded pleasantly but secretly wondered if he were raising the intensity of the watch he had decided to keep on her. Perhaps Dewhurst's call had worried him more than she'd realized. She waited while he went into the main cottage and found a fresh shirt to replace the dirt- and sweat-stained one he'd been wearing. He came out of the front door buttoning it.

"We'll take the Jeep," Flint said. He glanced down at Zipp who was sitting in the doorway. The cat looked up expectantly. "You're going to have to stay here, Zipp. Keep an eye on things for us." Flint closed the cat inside the house and locked the front door. "What have you got planned for dinner?" he asked Rani, automatically checking the lock.

"Sometimes I think you have a one-track mind." She followed him to the Jeep and climbed in beside him.

"Two tracks," he corrected with a grin as he turned the key in the Jeep's ignition.

"Food and sex?"

"I like to keep life simple."

He guided the Jeep out onto the narrow road that led toward the town of Reed Lake. Rani liked his driving. He brought to it the same competent, relaxed skill he brought to his gardening. She studied him out of the corner of her eye as he maneuvered the vehicle along the twisting, winding road. There were so many things she still didn't know about the man. How was it possible that he had so easily captured her heart when she had guarded it so carefully for so long?

"What are you thinking?" Flint demanded, shifting gears for a curve.

Rani moved restlessly in the seat and glanced out the window. "That it looks as though it's going to rain this evening." It was only a small lie, after all. And it did look as though a storm were brewing. The sky had been gray and overcast all day. Now the clouds seemed heavier, and the wind was definitely chilly. She should have brought along a jacket.

Flint found a space in front of the Reed Lake Post Office and followed Rani inside. Mrs. Hobson looked at both of them with interest as she handed over Rani's small stack of mail.

"Not much today, I'm afraid. How are things going out at the Anderson place?" the older woman inquired cheerfully. She looked from one to the other, obviously trying to determine just what was happening at the Anderson place.

"Fine, thank you." Rani flipped through the letters, ignoring the woman's curiosity. Mrs. Hobson wasn't going to rest until she had established the facts of the situation. Let her guess, Rani thought. It'll give her something to do. She wondered if she and Flint were providing the chief source of entertainment and speculation for the folks of Reed Lake these days. There wasn't all that much to do in the town.

Mrs. Hobson was persistent, however. She smiled brightly up at Flint. "That's a nice ring, Rani has. Did you give it to her?"

"No." Flint's total lack of interest was barely concealed behind a semblance of politeness. "It's a family ring."

"Oh, I see." Mrs. Hobson's obvious satisfaction made Rani smile. The woman had been fishing to find out just how scandalous the situation was at the Anderson place. Now she knew the ring was not a symbol of an engagement. That would make whatever was going on that much more interesting. "It's a lovely stone," Mrs. Hobson observed.

"Thank you." Rani picked up her mail.

"Not real, is it? I mean, an emerald that large...?"

Rani chuckled. "No, it's not real. Nicely cut glass."

Mrs. Hobson frowned thoughtfully, her interest switching from gossip to something of a more professional nature. "Glass? Mind if I take a closer look? I wouldn't have guessed it was glass. Perhaps another sort of green gem. There are plenty of green-colored stones besides emeralds, you know. Few of them have such good color, though."

Rani shrugged and slipped the ring off her finger. She handed it over the counter. Mrs. Hobson whipped out the jeweler's loupe, which she kept next to her collection of quartz. She popped it onto her glasses over her right eye and peered down at the object in her hand. "Hmmm."

"What do you think, Mrs. Hobson?" Rani asked indulgently.

There was a long silence while Mrs. Hobson studied the ring. At last she looked up, frowning in concentration. "You're quite sure this isn't an emerald?"

Rani's pulse suddenly picked up speed. Behind her she could feel Flint's almost palpable alertness. "I was told it was paste."

"Well, I'm no expert," Mrs. Hobson said, "but I can tell you for certain this isn't glass."

"Perhaps another sort of green stone?" Rani suggested carefully.

"If I had to take a bet," Mrs Hobson said casually, "I'd say it was a genuine emerald."

Rani realized she had forgotten to breathe for a few seconds. Flint was silent. Slowly Rani extended her hand and took back the ring. "Good heavens, Mrs. Hobson. If you really think there's a possibility it's genuine, perhaps I'd better get it reappraised."

"Wouldn't hurt. Unless you're quite sure of the facts," Mrs. Hobson said with a quick nod.

"No, I'm not absolutely positive of the facts. As Flint said, it's a family ring and everyone just assumed it was fake."

"I could be wrong, of course," Mrs. Hobson remarked. "After all, my specialty is quartz. But it might be a good idea to have a real jeweler take a look at it."

"Thank you, Mrs. Hobson. I believe I'll do that." Rani turned blindly and nearly collided with Flint. He reached out to steady her, his gaze intent.

"We still have to stop by the grocery store," he reminded her. "Good-bye, Mrs. Hobson." He guided Rani outside where the smell of rain was now in the air. "Don't look so shocked," he drawled. "If the ring is real, it would explain a lot of things."

"It doesn't explain why Charles Dewhurst told me it was paste."

"No," Flint said thoughtfully. "It doesn't."

They stopped at the grocery store to allow Rani to collect frozen ravioli and the makings for a cheese sauce. It was starting to sprinkle by the time they returned to the Jeep. Rani sat on the passenger side, studying the ring on her hand.

"I don't see any green fire," she complained.

"What green fire?" Flint swung the Jeep back onto the road.

"Dewhurst said that in a true emerald the inner light was quite striking. He said it was like looking into green fire."

"Maybe a gem expert sees things in stones the rest of us don't," Flint suggested dryly. "Or maybe he lied."

"Yes. Maybe he lied." Rani turned her head. "But why would he do that, Flint?"

"I don't know."

"If he'd been after the emerald he could have stolen it when I gave the ring to him to be valued."

"How? As soon as you discovered the loss you would have known exactly who'd stolen it. How long did he have Ambrose's collection?"

"Not long. Just for one afternoon."

Flint thought about it. "He wouldn't have had time to duplicate the emerald. No, he didn't have any choice except to give the ring back to you."

"Why tell me it was a fake?" she demanded. Then she came up with an answer to her own question. "Unless he didn't want me to think it was valuable. That way if I should happen to 'lose' it, I wouldn't make too big a fuss."

"Yeah. An interesting notion."

"Flint, I've got news for you. I don't find it interesting at all. I find it scary."

"You're not the only one," he responded grimly as he swung the Jeep around a curve.

"What do we do now?" Rani asked.

"I think we'd better see about getting the police involved. I'm not sure what they can do. There still isn't much to go on, but maybe they'll have some ideas. We're sure as hell going to get that ring off your hand and into a safe-deposit box."

The rain was beginning to fall in earnest by the time Flint pulled the Jeep into the driveway of the front cottage. "Wait here until I get the front door open or you'll get soaked

waiting on the porch," he said, reaching into the back seat
for one of the bags of groceries. "I've got to do something
about that leaking porch roof."

Hoisting the bag in one hand, Flint hurried up the steps
of the porch, flipped through the keys on his chain and
shoved the appropriate one into the lock.

He stopped dead on the threshold, realizing that the key
had found no resistance. The door was already unlocked.

The next thing he noticed was that Zipp wasn't waiting
impatiently on the other side of the door. The third thing he
noticed was the odd silence in the cottage. Everything felt
wrong.

"Stay where you are, Rani," he called very casually. "I'll
bring an umbrella."

She had one leg out of the Jeep and was waiting with a
grocery bag in her arms to make the dash for the house.
"It's all right, Flint, I don't mind getting a little wet."

"I said, stay there." This time he put enough command
into the words to make her blink. Setting the bag down on
the porch, he loped down the short flight of steps and over
to the Jeep. When he grabbed her arm, she looked up at him
in astonishment. She was opening her mouth to protest the
high handed action, but he already had her out of the Jeep.

"Flint, the groceries!" The bag fell from her arm, falling onto the wet, graveled drive. A can of tuna fish rolled
under the wheel of the Jeep. "What in the world? What do
you think you're doing?"

Flint ignored the confused demands. He was already
running, dragging her along with him into the shelter of the
surrounding woods. "Don't argue. Just move, Rani."

He sent up a silent prayer of thanks when she closed her
mouth and obeyed. Flint didn't slow until they were into a
stand of old fir. Huge branches cascaded to the ground like
the skirts of formal ball gowns. He sought temporary ref-

uge behind one grand dame. Rani was panting as he brought her to a halt. She looked questioningly up at him, her eyes wide with a silent demand for answers. The rain was pelting down heavily. Both of them were already quite wet. There was no sound from the direction of the cottage.

"Zipp didn't come to the door," Flint said starkly.

"So what? He often doesn't come to the door when there are strangers around—" She broke off, looking shaken as the full implications came home to her. "Oh, my God. I see what you mean. But, Flint, he might be outside or something."

"In this rain? You know cats and rain. Besides, I realized when I put the key in the lock that the door was already open."

"I remember you locking it," she whispered. "Do you think someone's been inside the cottage?"

"I think there's a possibility that someone has not only searched it, but that he's still in there. That's why Zipp is in hiding somewhere."

She stiffened under his hand. "I've heard you're not supposed to walk in on burglars. They tend to panic and get violent. But, Flint, by now whoever's in there must know we're gone. Why hasn't he come out? Where's his car? Maybe he's already left."

"I have a feeling he's still in there." Flint could barely see the corner of the porch when he peered through the branches of the old fir. "Stay here, Rani. I'm going back to have a look."

"The hell you are," she retorted. "We're both getting out of here."

He felt a stab of amusement at the sharpness of her tone. "You're cute when you're giving orders. I like to think it's because you care."

"Flint, I'm not joking. We have to get out of here and get the sheriff if you think there's a chance someone's in the house."

"I want to make a try for something that, like an idiot, I left behind."

"What? The groceries? Don't be ridiculous, Flint."

"Not the groceries. The gun. It's in the Jeep."

"Oh, my God. Flint, I don't think that's a good idea."

He glanced at her, debating how much to tell her. There wasn't time to go into details, and if he told her what he suspected she would only be more alarmed than she already was. How could he explain that he didn't think whoever was in the cottage would allow them to casually walk back to Reed Lake to get help?

"I'll be right back, Rani. Don't move."

She tightened her lips but said nothing. Flint patted her hand a little awkwardly and then slipped out from the cover of the huge fir. Hugging the shelter of the trees, he approached the house from an oblique angle. He tried to avoid coming into full view of anyone who might have been watching from a window.

But the last few yards between himself and the Jeep were devoid of any cover. He had to choose between making a dash for the driver's side or giving up the project altogether. Silently Flint crouched close to the ground, studying the quiet house and wondering if he was the victim of an overactive imagination. There was no movement from within. It was the unnatural stillness that bothered him the most. It was a waiting kind of stillness.

A hunter's stillness.

Flint made his decision. He ran for the Jeep, heading for the cover of the driver's side. The rifle shot cracked overhead just as he broke cover. Whirling in midair, Flint threw himself back into the trees, hitting the ground hard.

So much for the heroic dash to the Jeep. There was no way he could cross that open ground without getting shot. Accepting the inevitable, he picked himself up and ran back to where he had left Rani. Behind him he thought he heard the front door of the cottage open.

Flint saw a splash of color before he saw Rani and groaned silently as he realized her bright coral shirt was as vivid as a beacon. She was waiting with anxious eyes as he came through the low-hanging branches. He paused only long enough to grab her arm and start running again.

Rani felt his fingers close around her upper arm and staggered awkwardly to her feet. "No gun?"

"No gun."

"I heard that rifle shot. It wasn't just a hunter's shot, was it?"

"It was a hunter, all right, but not the usual kind. Get that shirt off, Rani."

She glanced down at herself. "But, Flint..."

"You can see it for yards. Don't you have any neutral colors in your wardrobe?"

"No."

"Get it off."

She fumbled frantically with the buttons as she ran. "Where are we going? The road?"

"Too obvious. If there was more traffic we might stand a chance of getting someone's attention, but I haven't heard a single car go by since we got back here. Let me have the shirt."

Mutely she tugged it off, vividly conscious of the lacy scrap of her bra. The rain was cold as it hit her bare skin. Flint took the bright shirt from her hand just as they topped a small rise and started down toward a tiny meadow filled with ancient, twisted manzanita shrubs.

They slowed, sticking to the edge of the meadow as they circled it. On the far side Flint stopped.

"What now?" Rani asked, glancing anxiously back through the woods. She could see nothing. Between the heavy rain and the thick stands of fir and pine, visibility was severely impaired. One could be grateful. "Do you think he's following us?"

"It's what I would do if I were in his shoes." Flint was arranging the coral shirt in the branches of a fir.

"Maybe he won't be able to figure out which way we've gone. This rain will make it hard to track us," Rani pointed out.

"We're going to have to assume he's a professional."

"A professional what?" she gasped. "Killer?"

"If he's not a professional, he'll be desperate. Either way, he'll be coming after us. He must realize by now that I'm not armed." Flint finished his work with the shirt and led Rani deeper into the woods. They crouched down in a small dip in the ground that was ringed by trees. Rani felt wet needles sticking unpleasantly into her bare skin. The small bra offered no protection from the elements or the terrain.

"Now what?" Rani asked again. She seemed to be asking that a lot today.

"Now we wait."

It occurred to Rani that the guy with the rifle wasn't the only professional in the vicinity. She cast a quick, curious glance at Flint's hard profile. He knew what he was doing and that was a frightening thought in and of itself.

"How long do we wait?" she asked quietly.

"Hush, Rani. Not another word." He pulled away from her, signaling her to stay put.

She watched as he slithered across the wet needles, realizing he was doubling back to the far side of the meadow. Holding herself very still, Rani tried to ignore the coldness of the rain and the way the green stone on her hand seemed to mock her.

The silence stretched out with unmerciful tension, broken only by the ceaseless drumming of the rain in the trees. The world seemed composed entirely of green and gray. Dusk was settling slowly, augmented by the weather. Visibility was becoming worse by the minute.

Rani was beginning to wonder if the horrible afternoon would ever end when she heard the crack of the rifle. The sound jolted her. She hugged herself tightly as another shot echoed through the storm.

The second shot was followed by a shout of mingled anger and surprise. Startled, Rani lifted her head and stared through the trees in the direction of the meadow. Two men were on the ground on the far side, twisting in a tangle of arms and legs. She knew at once what had happened.

When the gunman had paused at the edge of the manzanita meadow, he must have caught sight of the coral shirt among the branches. He'd gotten off two shots before Flint had jumped him.

There was an eerie absence of sound from the two men as they flailed savagely on the ground. Frantically Rani dashed forward into the meadow and across it.

She arrived in time to see Flint straddle his opponent and launch a brutal fist straight into Mike Slater's jaw. Slater's eyes rolled back into his head, and his body went very still.

Ten

Don't say it," Flint ordered as Rani followed him out of the trees and back into the driveway of the cottage.

"Say what?" she demanded.

"That he seemed like such a nice man."

"Well, he did. A very pleasant, artistic type. I liked him, Flint."

"With one glaring exception, you've got lousy taste in men."

She grinned in spite of herself. "Who's the glaring exception?"

"Me."

"Oh, of course." She sobered thoughtfully. "Do you think he'll be okay tied up back there with our belts?"

"Are you afraid he'll drown in this rain?"

Rani thought of the unconscious man Flint had left secured in the woods. "I wasn't worried about that. I was just afraid he might get away."

"It would take him hours to work through those belts even if he wakes up in a condition to make the effort. We'll be back with the authorities by then." Flint glanced around the yard. He was carrying Slater's rifle with the same casual expertise he used to drive the Jeep or work in the garden. "I don't see Zipp."

"He probably hightailed it when Slater walked into the house. It might be sometime before he reappears." Rani straightened the soaking wet coral shirt she was wearing. "I'm cold, Flint. You must be freezing, too. Both of us need a shower."

"First I'm going to call the local authorities. There are a hell of a lot of questions that need answering. When Slater wakes up, I want those answers. You can take a shower while I'm on the phone." He shoved open the door and stood aside for her to enter.

Rani frowned up into his lean, lined face. "At least put on some dry clothing. I don't want you catching pneumonia."

A faint smile flared briefly in his green gaze. "Yes ma'am. Right after I call the sheriff's office."

She sighed and started down the hall. Flint could be as stubborn as Zipp at times. She was going to have to work at finding a suitable way of managing him. Currently her methods were too unreliable. Sometimes they worked and sometimes they didn't.

Rani rounded the corner of the bedroom and nearly collided with Charles Dewhurst.

He was clearly as rattled by the near collision as she was, but Dewhurst had a distinct advantage. He was holding a small pistol in one hand.

"Don't move!" he hissed in a sharp whisper, pointing the weapon at her as if it were a magic wand. "Don't move an inch."

Rani froze, her eyes going from the gun to Dewhurst's nervous but fiercely determined expression. "Mr. Dewhurst, I don't understand," she managed weakly. "What are you doing here?"

"Take a wild guess," he snapped. "Turn around and walk ahead of me down the hall."

"I'm getting sick and tired of guns being pointed in my direction."

"Shut up!" He prodded her with his gun as she reluctantly turned and started back down the hall to the living room.

There was no sound from the other room. Flint obviously hadn't had a chance to dial the sheriff's number yet. Even as she watched, he appeared silently at the far end of the hall, the rifle in his hand. She said nothing as Dewhurst prodded Rani again.

"I want the ring, of course," Dewhurst said tightly. He reached out and wrapped an arm around Rani's neck, pulling her back against him.

"Sure," Flint agreed quietly. "It was you all along, wasn't it? You're the mysterious man on the trail of the Clayborne ring. Did you hire Slater to do the dirty work back East as well as here?"

"He was a fool. I thought he knew what he was doing. But he failed both times. Oh, he managed to kill Ambrose, all right, but he didn't get the ring. The whole point was to get the ring. But Ambrose had already taken care to see that it was safe. I was so close and he beat me again. For years Ambrose and I have chased the Clayborne ring. When I learned he had finally gotten his hands on it, I couldn't believe it. He didn't deserve it. He had no right to it. He made his living *copying stones*, for God's sake. He made fakes. *Paste*. When he held the real thing in his hands his only interest was in duplicating it and selling the original. The man had no ability to appreciate true gems. What right did he have to something like the Clayborne ring? He wasn't worthy of that beautiful stone with all its history."

"After the screwup back East you had to bide your time, didn't you?" Flint murmured.

"It was a long wait, but it was worth it when I convinced Ambrose's heir to bring the collection to me to be valued. She thought I was merely doing her a favor! I saw at once that Ambrose hadn't had time or inclination to copy the ring. Once I knew where it was again I could take my time planning a way to get it. Put down that rifle or I'll kill her, Cottrell. Go on, put it down."

Slowly Flint lowered the rifle, his eyes never leaving Dewhurst. "When Slater told you I was on the scene you couldn't figure out what was going on, could you? So you played a wild card and tried telling Rani someone was after the ring. You hoped she'd get scared and assume it was me."

"It would have been a logical assumption. As far as we could figure out, she didn't know much about you. After all, you're just a handyman."

"Yeah, I'm supposed to be that, all right."

Rani broke into the tense conversation. "Why did you tell me the ring was a fake, Dewhurst?"

"So you wouldn't panic and put it somewhere I couldn't get at it."

"Somewhere like a safe-deposit box?" she asked.

"Exactly. And you believed me. It was so easy. It was obvious you had no eye for the real thing. No appreciation for true beauty. You don't deserve the ring any more than Ambrose did. But I needed time to work out a way of getting it without drawing attention to myself. I thought at first the easiest thing to do was have Slater simply steal if from you. You'd never know who'd taken it, and since you assumed it was a fake you wouldn't get too concerned. But

Slater said he was just setting up the situation, just getting close to you, when *he* showed up." Dewhurst indicated Flint with an aggressive movement of his chin.

"So Slater suggested staging a hunting accident," Flint concluded.

"That was Mike shooting at me that day in the woods?" Rani was suddenly intensely angry.

"That incompetent couldn't even handle a simple hunting accident," Dewhurst raged. "When he blew that, I decided I'd better come up here and take charge. We've been biding our time, Slater and I. Waiting for an opportunity. Slater was supposed to take care of this end of things but, as usual, he obviously failed. Luckily I was prepared for that contingency."

Rani could hear the older man's breath coming too quickly in his chest. The arm around her neck was rigid with tension. She guessed he'd never been faced with dealing out real violence himself. It was a different proposition from that of hiring a professional such as Slater.

"Back up, Cottrell. Slowly. Back into the living room. Stay where I can keep an eye on you." Dewhurst hustled Rani ahead of him, still locking her close with his arm.

"It won't work, Dewhurst." Flint spoke calmly, as if discussing whether to plant roses or azaleas. "Slater has made too much of a mess of things. Your best bet is to get out of here. If I were you, I'd leave the country."

"There won't be any need for me to leave the country," Dewhurst said dangerously. "And I'm not going anywhere without the ring. I've searched for it too long. Take it off, Rani. Put it down on the table."

"I get the feeling you're going to kill us anyway, so why should I cooperate?"

"Damn you, you little bitch! Take off that ring. It's mine!"

Dewhurst tightened his hold around Rani's throat, shaking her in an excess of tension and fury. Rani staggered in his grasp. Dewhurst struggled to regain his balance. Out of the corner of her eye, Rani caught a flash of movement down around her feet. There was a startling screech that could only have come from an enraged cat, and Dewhurst jerked backward in instinctive reaction. He had stepped on Zipp's tail. Zipp dashed back into the kitchen where he'd been hiding.

Rani didn't hesitate. She could feel her captor struggling to rebalance himself. It was the only chance she was going to get. She swung her hand upward, palm out, and slashed the huge ring across the side of Dewhurst's face. The man yelled, twisting his head to avoid the painful swipe; Rani shoved at him and they both lost their balance.

The gun in Dewhurst's hand roared in Rani's ear, temporarily deafening her. She felt herself falling and then she was free of her tormentor's hold as Flint moved with lethal grace to end the chaotic scene.

Rani looked up at Flint from her position on the floor. He was pinning Charles Dewhurst's arms. Rani assayed a shaky smile that held her bubbling relief. "You're very useful around the house, Flint."

It seemed hours before the mess was cleared up to a reasonable extent. The authorities responded quickly enough, but it took time to go through the paperwork and to explain the bizarre situation. Rani and Flint did learn in the process that the man who had called himself Mike Slater was also known as Lawrence Carmichael and was wanted under that name in several states.

Rani and Flint had a late snack, which they shared with a disgruntled Zipp and they fell into bed. There was no passionate lovemaking that night. Both of them were asleep almost instantly. It wasn't until Rani stretched languidly awake in Flint's arms the next morning that she suspected something was wrong. He was wide awake, as usual, waiting quietly for her to open her eyes.

"What is it?" she asked softly, sensing a different sort of stillness in him that morning. She touched him lightly, aware of a tension within herself.

"I've been thinking."

Rani closed her eyes, afraid of what was coming. It was much too soon. Sooner than she had expected. But she would not cry. She had known this moment would arrive sooner or later and *she would not cry*. She had lived with the knowledge in the back of her mind since she had met Flint Cottrell. You couldn't hold a free-ranging alley cat if he didn't want to stay.

"I guess I was hoping for later," she whispered.

Flint shifted to look down at her. She felt his fingers under her chin lifting her face. Bravely she opened her eyes, her lashes damp with unshed tears.

"You're crying," he accused softly.

"No. I told myself I wouldn't cry."

"Please don't cry, Rani."

She tried a tiny smile. "I won't."

"What did you mean, you hoped for later?" he demanded urgently.

"I was hoping that you'd choose to hang around a while longer. I knew you'd leave sooner or later. I'd hoped for later."

He swore softly. "I knew it. That's exactly what I've been thinking about this morning. Damn it, Rani."

"It's all right, Flint. I'm a big girl and I've known all along what was coming. I was prepared for this when I took my risk."

"It is not all right," he snapped. "*I've* known all along you didn't trust me to stay. It's been driving me crazy."

"It's not a question of trust. It's a question of understanding," she protested gently. "I do understand, Flint. Honest."

"The hell you do. Listen to me, Rani Garroway, and listen good. I'm not leaving. I can't leave. I don't want to leave. Can't you get it through your stubborn little head that I'm home now? You couldn't get rid of me if you tried."

Frantically she tried to stifle the flare of hope that was threatening to overwhelm her. "You're not leaving now that you've done your duty by my uncle?"

"Now you're finally catching on. Rani, I came here because of a feeling that I owed Ambrose something. I'd been too late to protect him, but I thought I might be able to protect his niece. But that's not why I'm staying. I want a home with you, Rani. Now do you understand?"

She smiled tremulously. "Let's just say I'm more than willing to be convinced."

He sighed. "That's what I was thinking about just now. Convincing you."

"Oh, Flint, I didn't mean it that way," she said anxiously, terrified that he'd misunderstood her tiny attempt at lightness.

"No, you're absolutely right. You deserve to be convinced."

"Flint, wait a minute, you don't understand."

He shook his head, leaning back against the pillow. Rani recognized with dismay the stubborn, set expression in his emerald eyes. "I'm going to take the time to convince you, Rani. According to the legend of the ring, the other men who found themselves in my situation eventually took drastic action. They forced their women into marriage. But I'm not going to do it that way. This isn't a legend we're

living here, it's for real. I want things done properly. I don't
want to push you. I'll show you I know what I'm doing and
that I'm here to stay. I'll prove you can trust me."

"How?" She was deeply wary now.

"We'll go back to Santa Rosa, your town, your neighborhood. I'll get a regular job. A nine-to-five job. Something with a real desk and an office copier. A job with
benefit plans and retirement plans and sick leave. I can find
one. Hell, I can do just about anything. I'll show you I'm
capable of taking care of a family and that I've got the determination to stick around for the long haul. In a few
months, when I've settled into the routine and you're confident I'm not going to disappear in the middle of the night,
we'll get married. In a year or two, when you're really convinced I'm reliable, we can talk about having a kid. I'd like
a child, Rani, but I realize a woman has to be sure of a man
before she takes that kind of risk. All along I've wanted you
to take a risk on me, but I know it's not fair of me to ask you
to do that until I've given you some evidence that I'm going
to make a dependable husband and father."

"Flint . . ."

"The thing is, Rani," he went on very seriously, "we
really shouldn't wait too long to have a kid. I'm getting close
to forty and you've just turned thirty. Biological clocks and
all that stuff, you know. We won't be able to postpone it too
long. Do you think it will take too long for me to prove myself to you?"

Rani leaned over him, her eyes very brilliant with her love.
"Flint, there is absolutely no need to go through all of that.
If you say you're going to stay, that's all the proof I need. I
love you, Cottrell. I trust you." She brushed her mouth
against his, willing him to respond.

"I love you, Rani."

His voice was husky and weighted with emotion. Rani could have sworn there was a trace of dampness in the emerald fires of his eyes. The thought fascinated her. She nestled close, offering comfort and love as Flint's big hand stroked heavily through her tangled hair. He kissed her with a deep need and a promise that filled her with hope and trust in the future. He did love her. Rani was certain of it.

"Can we get married now?" she demanded teasingly as Flint slowly broke the kiss.

"In a few months," he said firmly. "When you're sure of me."

"Flint, please, there's no need for this."

"This is the best way, Rani."

"According to you! Flint, this is crazy," Rani said, knowing already she was virtually helpless against the stubborn streak in him.

"Trust me, Rani."

"I don't seem to have any choice," she said unhappily. "There's just one thing I won't tolerate, Flint Cottrell."

He smiled crookedly. "What's that?"

"No nine-to-five desk job for you. I can't see you behind a desk."

"What would you suggest?"

"I suggest," she said, "that you find a job doing what you do best."

Two months later Flint pushed open the small wrought-iron gate and started up the garden walk of his new home. He examined the gingerbread trim around the windows as he climbed the porch steps. He'd finished painting it the day before and was pleased with the way it looked. The next step was the plumbing. A man could devote a lifetime to plumbing repairs if he wasn't careful. But women were fussy about good plumbing. He couldn't ask Rani to move in until he got the kitchen remodeled and the new shower installed. Another month or two would give him time to take care of the basics. Then he could talk seriously to Rani about taking the risk of marrying him.

The old Victorian house had been in a very dilapidated condition when he'd found it. The owners had given him an incredible deal, and Flint had grabbed it. He was good at grabbing an opportunity when it arose. He'd moved out of his apartment and into the old house at once.

Flint liked the neighborhood. It wasn't far from Rani's place, and there was plenty of space around the house for a garden. He liked the town, too. Santa Rosa was a good size but not overcrowded. The mountains were near, and San Francisco could be reached in an hour's drive. A good town for raising kids and flowers. Flint stood on the porch, surveying his domain with a satisfied gaze. Everything was falling into place very nicely. Soon, another couple of months at most, everything would be perfect.

Rani had been persistent at first, trying everything from logic to tantrums to convince him to at least let her move in with him. But Flint had stood firm. He had insisted Rani stay in her own place during what he called his trial period. True, he saw her nearly every evening for dinner and frequently spent the night, but he thought he'd managed to keep the affair as free of outright coercion as possible. He wanted her to be sure of him. He wanted her to trust him completely before he took the final step. In another couple of months he thought she would have enough evidence of his new, domesticated ways.

Pleased with himself, Flint unlocked the front door, stepped inside the hall and nearly tripped over Zipp. The cat sat on his haunches, meowing quietly in welcome. Flint stood stock-still, staring down at the big animal.

"What are you doing here, Zipp?"

Before the cat could answer, Flint caught an aroma of a rich fish stew wafting down the hall from the old kitchen. Curiously he walked forward, Zipp at his heels.

"Rani?"

She looked up from the salad she was preparing on the cracked drainboard and smiled brilliantly. She was wearing a loud crimson-and-yellow sweater over a pair of black trousers and, as always, she looked sexy and sweet. God, how he loved her, Flint thought even as he narrowed his eyes in a reproving frown.

"Hello, Flint." She dropped the spinach leaves and came forward to kiss him lightly on the mouth. Then she returned industriously to her salad. "How are things at the nursery?"

"Fine. The shipment of Christmas trees arrived from that supplier in Reed Lake," he said automatically. "Just in time. And we got the fancy tulip bulbs from Holland today. I've got a long line of customers waiting for them." He directed his gaze pointedly at the salad. "Rani, what are you doing here? We're supposed to have dinner at your place tonight. I just came home to change my clothes."

She scanned his dirt-stained jeans. "Yes, why don't you do that? You've got potting soil all over you." She began slicing mushrooms. "I'll pour us both a glass of wine while you're washing up."

He hesitated, aware of a distinct feeling of being gently manipulated. This was the first time Rani had cooked a meal in his new house. The place wasn't ready for her. Unable to think of quite what to do about the change of plans, Flint decided the simplest thing was to wash up as she had instructed. He went down the hall to the bathroom.

Stepping inside, he realized Rani had changed more than just the evening's dinner plans. There was a new toothbrush standing beside his own in the glass that sat on the chipped sink. When he opened the cabinet, he found an array of feminine items inside that certainly didn't belong to him. He stood scowling at a pink deodorant bottle and then slowly shut the cabinet door.

He washed the traces of rich soil from his hands. Running a large professional nursery was a dirty business, but the dirt was clean. Not like some of the dirt he'd had on his hands during his former life. He'd fallen into the nursery management job with his usual luck. A little fast talking and some convincing displays of his gardening skills, as well as his management skills, had persuaded the owner, Mr. Rodriguez, that he knew what he was doing. Once he'd been sure Rani wholeheartedly approved of the work and didn't find it "unprofessional," Flint had launched into the job with enthusiasm. Now Rodriguez was talking about retiring. He had inquired that day if his new manager was interested in purchasing the business. Terms could be worked out. He was a flexible man. Flint hadn't hesitated, he'd said yes immediately. Owning the nursery would speed up the approach of the day when he would feel he had a right to ask Rani to marry and move in with him. His new life was falling into place the way he'd planned.

Flint realized he thought of his life in two segments now—BR and AR. Before Rani and After Rani. He didn't waste time dwelling on the BR portion of his existence. Rani and the future were all that mattered.

Flint rinsed his hands and eyed the rest of the bathroom. Rani's hairbrush was sitting on the counter along with a red plastic comb. He dried his rough palms on a towel and left the bathroom for the bedroom. A suspicion was growing steadily in his mind.

When he opened the closet doors, he knew he was right. To the right of his drab collection of work shirts and pants hung an array of brightly colored blouses, skirts and blazers. Underneath them was a neat row of sandals and high-heeled shoes. Flint just stood there, staring, until he sensed Rani at the doorway behind him.

Slowly he turned to look at her. "You've moved in."

She nodded once, her mouth set in a determined line, although there was a faint wariness in her eyes. She held the salad tongs in front of her as if in self-defense. "I've waited long enough. I decided to use your own technique and not ask for permission. If we do things your way we might go on waiting another couple of months. I'm not interested in waiting any longer. I love you, Flint, and you love me. It's high time we got married."

"I wanted you to be sure of me. I didn't want you to think you had to take a risk on me."

She smiled and stepped forward, putting her arms around his neck. "I suppose you could say that just living day to day is a series of risks. I've decided some risks are much more interesting than others, however. I've waited a long time to find a man who's worth taking a chance on. Now that I've found him, I'm afraid there's hardly any risk involved at all. You, Flint Cottrell, are a sure thing."

"Do you really believe that, Rani?" He wrapped his arms around her, aware that his hands were trembling slightly.

"With all my heart," she whispered.

"Rani." He caught her face between his palms and kissed her with rough eagerness. "Rani, I swear I won't let you down. Ever."

"I know," she said simply. "I swear I won't ever let you down, either."

When Flint lifted his mouth from hers at last, his emerald eyes were gleaming. Rani looked wonderingly into their depths.

"Green fire," she murmured.

"What are you talking about?" he asked with sensual humor.

"Dewhurst said that in real emeralds there was a green fire that captured anyone who looked deeply into the stones." She had to admit she'd never really seen anything that qualified as fire in the Clayborne ring that presently resided in a safe-deposit box, but when she looked into Flint's eyes she believed what Charles Dewhurst had said. "He was right."

When spring arrived the old Victorian house was looking very pleased with itself. It had just about everything a house could want. There was a large cat who spent most of his time dozing on the freshly painted porch, a man and a woman who filled the inside with passion and love, and a truly spectacular garden. Neighbors always stopped to gaze at the velvet lawn and the unbelievable wealth of plants and flowers. Everyone agreed that the Cottrell garden was the marvel of the neighborhood.

The article Flint Cottrell had written on the Clayborne ring was published in the August issue of *Legends and Fantasy* that year. The popular magazine hit the stands the same day that Amanda Jane Cottrell was born. She didn't know it then, but her proud parents planned to give her a very special ring when she grew up. It had a brilliant green stone in it that would match her eyes.

OFFICIAL SWEEPSTAKES INFORMATION

1. **NO PURCHASE NECESSARY.** To enter, complete the official entry/ order form. Be sure to indicate whether or not you wish to take advantage of our subscription offer.

2. Entry blanks have been pre-selected for the prizes offered. Your response will be checked to see if you are a winner. In the event that these are not claimed, a random drawing will be held from all entries received to award not less than $150,000 in prizes. This is in addition to any free, surprise or mystery gifts which might be offered. Versions of this sweepstakes with different prizes will appear in Torstar Ltd. mailings and their affiliates. Winners selected will receive the prize offered in their sweepstakes insert.

3. This promotion is being conducted under the supervision of Marden-Kane, an independent judging organization. By entering the sweepstakes, each entrant accepts and agrees to be bound by these rules and the decisions of the judges which shall be final and binding. Odds of winning in the random drawing are dependent upon the total number of entries received. Taxes, if any, are the sole responsibility of the prize winners. Prizes are non-transferable. All entries must be received by August 31, 1986.

4. This sweepstakes package offers:

1, Grand Prize	: Cruise around the world on the QEII	$ 100,000 total value
4, First Prizes	: Set of matching pearl necklace and earrings	$ 20,000 total value
10, Second Prizes	: Romantic Weekend in Bermuda	$ 15,000 total value
25, Third Prizes	: Designer Luggage	$ 10,000 total value
200, Fourth Prizes	: $25 Gift Certificate	$ 5,000 total value
		$150,000

Winners may elect to receive the cash equivalent for the prizes offered.

5. This offer is open to residents of the U.S. and Canada, 18 years and older, except employees of Torstar Ltd., its affiliates, subsidiaries, Marden-Kane and all other agencies and persons connected with conducting this sweepstakes. All Federal, State and local laws apply. Void in the province of Quebec and wherever prohibited or restricted by law. Winners will be notified by mail and may be required to execute an affidavit of eligibility and release which must be returned within 14 days after notification. Canadian winners will be required to answer a skill testing question. Winners consent to the use of their names, photograph and/or likeness for advertising and publicity purposes in conjunction with this and similar promotions without additional compensation. One prize per family or household.

6. For a list of our most current prize winners, send a stamped, self-addressed envelope to: WINNERS LIST, c/o Marden-Kane, P.O. Box 10404, Long Island City, New York 11101.

SSR-A-1

AMERICAN TRIBUTE

Where a man's dreams count for more than his parentage...

Look for these upcoming titles under the Special Edition American Tribute banner.

CHEROKEE FIRE
Gena Dalton #307—May 1986
It was Sabrina Dante's silver spoon that Cherokee cowboy Jarod Redfeather couldn't trust. The two lovers came from opposite worlds, but Jarod's Indian heritage taught them to overcome their differences.

NOBODY'S FOOL
Renee Roszel #313—June 1986
Everyone bet that Martin Dante and Cara Torrence would get together. But Martin wasn't putting any money down, and Cara was out to prove that she was nobody's fool.

MISTY MORNINGS, MAGIC NIGHTS
Ada Steward #319—July 1986
The last thing Carole Stockton wanted was to fall in love with another politician, especially Donnelly Wakefield. But under a blanket of secrecy, far from the campaign spotlights, their love became a powerful force.

AMERICAN TRIBUTE

*American Tribute titles
now available:*

RIGHT BEHIND THE RAIN
Elaine Camp #301—April 1986
The difficulty of coping with her brother's
death brought reporter Raleigh Torrence
to the office of Evan Younger, a police
psychologist. He helped her to deal with
her feelings and emotions, including love.

THIS LONG WINTER PAST
Jeanne Stephens #295—March 1986
Detective Cody Wakefield checked out
Assistant District Attorney Liann McDowell,
but only in his leisure time. For it was the
danger of Cody's job that caused Liann to
shy away.

LOVE'S HAUNTING REFRAIN
Ada Steward #289—February 1986
For thirty years a deep dark secret kept them
apart—King Stockton made his millions while
his wife, Amelia, held everything together.
Now could they tell their secret, could they
admit their love?